Timeless

By Alexandra Layos

Saddle & Bridle, Inc.

Dedication
To Team Sweigart, and in turn Team Leroy, for even now,
they remain one and the same.

Saddle & Bridle, Inc.
375 Jackson Avenue
St. Louis, Missouri 63130
www.saddleandbridle.com
(314) 725-9115

ISBN
0-9655501-4-1
Library of Congress Catalog Card Number: Pending
Manufactured in the United States of America

Thanks

A big thank you goes out to Traveler, a great jumper who overcame huge odds, and whose story inspired my own story which you now hold in your hands. To Dr. Annemarie Yoder DVM, for her veterinary expertise; without her guidance, Major's leg would have never healed! To my wonderful artist, Sarah, for bringing to life what even the power of words could not. To Mr. Jeffrey Thompson, my publisher, who always believed. And, once again, a thank you to Leroy, my inspiration...

Table of Contents

The People

Maria: A freshman in high school, who rides and shows with Sunny Ridge Stables. She owns a 3-gaited American Saddlebred, named Sultan, and was the one to figure out the mystery about Night Watch in The Missing Link. She was Angel's former owner, and is Emily's best friend.

Emily: Maria's best friend who owns Angel, and was involved in all of her adventures. She moved to Sunny Ridge when her barn moved to Kentucky.

Sally: The trainer at Sunny Ridge Stables.

Carol: Huntseat rider, who has a terrible accident riding Major and blames herself.

Jessica: Maria's step-mother, who began riding in an attempt to make Maria like her better, but immediately fell in love with the sport. She owns and shows Timmy.

Anne Dorman: Emily's older sister, who has just graduated from college. She owns Triumph.

Eric, Tina, Sam, and Christine: All teenagers of about the same age who ride at Sunny Ridge.

Amanda: A new rider at Sunny Ridge, who just switched to Saddleseat. She owns a Morgan named Holiday.

Claire: A young rider at Sunny Ridge who has been riding Saddleseat her entire life. She has been riding lesson horses while her parents and Sally search for a good horse she can show in Walk and Trot.

Tara: Young rider who is new to Sunny Ridge and riding, but soon becomes Claire's best friend.

Rachel: Assistant trainer at Sunny Ridge.

Jeff: Carol's husband.

The Horses

Major (Timeless): American Saddlebred; liver chestnut gelding. Originally huntseat, until he sustains a serious injury.

Sultan (CH My Majesty): American Saddlebred; black 3-gaited gelding owned by Maria.

Angel (Only Angel): American Saddlebred; grey park mare owned by Emily.

Timmy (As Time Goes By): American Saddlebred; bay 3-gaited gelding, owned by Jessica.

Triumph (Midnight Triumph): Hackney Pony; black harness mare, owned by Anne.

Holiday: Morgan; owned by Amanda.

Sly: American Saddlebred; chestnut (former) five-gaited gelding. Claire takes lessons on him.

Chapter 1

Sometimes unexpected things happen, and the way they happen leaves awed onlookers standing in disbelief. This was one of those times. His chocolate coat shimmered in the brightly lit arena, and his smooth rocking canter propelled them around the ring. She sat deep, guided him through the jumps that were set up, as the announcer called their name and number over the loudspeaker. She smiled. The crowd loved him. She touched him with her leg and they were off, powerful strides eating up the ground, yet he was the picture of grace; nimble like a dancer. Taking the first jump in perfect style, they headed toward the second. She could feel the horse's excitement, his power as they touched down and galloped to the third. A quick turn, then the in-and-out. He was totally focused. He loved to jump, loved to show, and always put his whole heart into the performance. Unlike most top jumpers though, he was a Saddlebred. He had competed against the best— and won. He had changed the common misconception many people held about Saddlebreds and what they were capable of. No one could dispute his talent. She felt his strength and held it in. Not yet, not yet. No faster now. Easy does it. She guided him around the last turn and let him loose. He flew down the center to the last jump. He would need some momentum on this one, it was big, and he knew it too. He was at his best, ears forward, *excitement building with every stride…he was lifting off, but something wasn't quite right. As he soared upwards, something from outside the ring caught his attention. A loud bang, and in that second his concentration snapped, and his back legs hit the jump. He landed, twisted, and stumbled, nearly going down. His rider was thrown clear over his head and hit the ground a few feet away as the crowd's gasp turned to a deadly hush.*

RING RING RING! I stood near the phone at the barn, Sultan's bridle in one hand, leg wraps, girth, and splint boots under my arm. With my other I was attempting to reach for the kimberwick bit which was kept on a top hook on the wall. I glanced around me, and seeing no one else present, I sighed, shoved most of my armload under my left elbow, and went to retrieve the phone. "Hello, Sunny Ridge Stables."

"Uh, hello, is Sally Adams around?" a man's voice asked.

"I think she's up giving a lesson right now. Would you like to leave a message? Or, if it's important I could go get her."

"Would you, please?" the man seemed relieved.

"Sure."

I quickly hung up the bridle and dropped all of my things on the ground. I raced up to the outdoor ring where Sally was giving a lesson to Valerie on Champ.

"Sally!" I called. "There's a phone call for you! It's important."

"Okay, I'm coming." She waved, said something to Valerie, and headed down to the barn. I returned to my previous spot, retrieved the bridle, and snatched the kimberwick bit down from its hook. I changed it with the mule bit currently in his work bridle and grabbed my arm load of stuff that I had dropped. In the process, I overheard part of Sally's frantic conversation on the phone. "Oh my gosh, is she okay? How's Major?" A long pause. "Oh, shoot." After another second she asked, "What hospital is she in? Can I come see her?" That caught my ears. Who was in the hospital? And who was Major? "Okay," she got out a piece of paper and wrote something down. I was about to leave when

I heard the next line and paused. "Well where's he going to go? Yeah, I do have an empty stall. Just the coffin bone? That's pretty bad though." I glanced at her out of the corner of my eye. She was talking about a horse. "Alright, then. How about I call you back later after my last lesson and we figure this out?" Her mother walked in at that moment.

"Who's she talking to?" she whispered to me.

"I don't know," I confessed.

"Alright, Jeff. Hang in there. Bye." Sally hung up the phone. She turned to her mother. "That was Carol's husband, Jeff. Carol was at a show with Major yesterday and at the last jump both of them had a bad fall. She's alright; she's in the hospital with a few broken bones, a concussion, and one really nasty blow to one of her legs…can't remember which; Major broke a coffin bone. Jeff wanted to know if we could keep him here until Carol recovers. I mean, Jeff isn't a horse person. He's not going to take care of him. I told him yes, of course."

"They really think he'll recover?"

"No, they really don't. Jeff just doesn't want to make any decisions alone. He's Carol's horse. I mean, it's not impossible, but it's highly unlikely. Most people don't even give them the chance because it's such a long road and horses just can't deal with it. It takes a certain temperament to be cooped up for so long. Even if he did recover, I doubt he'd ever jump again." She shook her head. Her mother nodded.

"We do have an empty stall. Wow, that's such a shame, though. That was one darn good horse. I haven't met many horses that impressed me like that one did." She chuckled a bit. "A Saddlebred jumper, headed for the top ranks of jumping."

"A Saddlebred?" I jumped into the conversation. She nodded.

"Yeah, a Saddlebred. His name was Timeless. I remember him as a weanling. He was shown in-hand at Louisville as a baby. Carol was there with us that year helping out, and fell in love with him. She bought him with the intention of showing him Saddleseat. Once his jumping talent showed though, what else was there to do? She had ridden huntseat before Sally introduced her to Saddleseat, so it was no big change for her. Oh, he was spectacular. I think there's a photo of him in the album upstairs..." she added as an afterthought. I nodded, gathered my things, dropped them in front of Sultan's stall and went up the stairs to get my saddle.

I noticed the photo album sitting there, staring at me, and I couldn't help but open it to get a glimpse of the horse that sounded so spectacular. Indeed, on the last page there was a collage of photos of a big liver chestnut Saddlebred gelding, flying over jumps, parked out in a show pose, and prancing in a ring full of jumps. He was absolutely gorgeous, and darn he looked like a good jumper. I'd known American Saddlebreds were versatile, but I'd never heard of one that beat all the warmbloods and Thoroughbreds in jumping. It was common knowledge that Thoroughbreds and warmbloods were the breeds best suited for it. I closed the book. I didn't even know the horse, and was thinking that it really was a shame.

I picked up my saddle and headed down to Sultan. My black gelding raised his head and came to the door when he saw me, so I slid on his halter, backed him up and cross-tied him. "You ready to ride, boy?" I questioned, patting his muscular neck. He turned his black face toward me and nudged my shoulder. "I guess so," I laughed, leaning my cheek against his face, and for a moment we stood there in silence before I stepped back to gather grooming supplies. I strolled over to the community box of supplies and then back to his stall. I curried and brushed his coat, and when I was done returned everything to the box on the shelf.

Sultan was standing with his ears forward, eyes bright, waiting expectantly when I returned. I reached for the leg wraps and rolled them onto his front legs, strapped the splint boots on his back legs, and settled the saddle pad on his back. He sidestepped as I was lifting up my saddle. One step forward and two steps backwards and to the right on a diagonal. Always. "Whoa, Sultan," I commanded, as always. I set it down and began to buckle the girth. One hole, two holes, three… "I'll get the rest later," I muttered, "once you let your breath out." He snorted. "Yeah, I know, you have it so hard. It's terrible." This time he snorted all over me. "Thanks." As I was wiping off my shirt Amanda came around the corner holding a bridle belonging to Holiday, her Morgan gelding. Holiday and Amanda were new to Sunny Ridge, and she would be riding with me during my lesson time today. "Hey, Amanda." I straightened up.

"Hey," she held out her bridle. "This thing is kind of complicated. Would you help me put it on?" It was a show bridle, the Saddleseat kind with two bits, four reins, and a curb chain. I laughed.

"Sure." She and Holiday had formerly competed in western and had won some big Morgan shows together, but apparently she had never shown Saddleseat before! "Not used to a double bridle, huh?" I asked.

"No, I've had friends who've ridden Saddleseat, but I've never done it. After years of everyone coming up to me and telling me what a great English Pleasure horse Holiday would make, I decided to give it a try. I just bought this bridle, and Sally wanted to see how it fit," she said, fingering the stiff, new leather. I stepped forward and took the bridle from her, and together we walked to Holiday's stall. I'd watched Sally long-line him the other day. He was a perky little bay with lots of motion for a western horse. I couldn't wait to see him when his feet grew out…I unclipped one cross-tie, slid off his halter, and put the reins over Holiday's head. Then, as Amanda watched, I held the caveson up, near the headstall with my right hand, gathered both bits in my left, slid them into his mouth, pulled the headstall over his ears and dropped the cavesson down, all in one motion. I arranged the cavesson, throatlatch and curb chain, and fixed his forelock just so, tucking it to the right side. I straightened the bits in his mouth, and handed her the reins. "There you go. It's not really that complicated once you get used to it." I smiled.

"Thanks," she replied gratefully. I made my way back to Sultan's stall and quickly bridled him. "Let's go boy." He followed me down the aisle.

Out in the ring I asked Sultan to park out, and I rolled down my stirrups. Hooking up my draw reins, I glanced around at Sally who was walking toward me. "Hey," she said, reaching for Sultan's bridle as I tightened the girth. "What's new with you?"

"Oh, not much," I stepped back, glanced over at her.

"You ready?" she asked me. I nodded.

"One, two, three...up!" She hoisted me into the saddle with the normal routine. I collected my reins, found my stirrups, and clucked to the big horse beneath me as Sally made her way over to Amanda and Holiday. Sultan moved out toward the rail, already dancing beneath me, ears forward, excitedly refusing to walk. "Can't you just flat walk for the first trip around?" I asked irritably. I lowered my hands to his withers, repeated "Walk" firmly, touching and releasing the bridle. I felt his energy building, building, and knew soon it would burst...he did a half-rear, and spun to the left, dancing sideways and snorting all the while.

"Excuse me, what was that?" Sally asked, turning toward us from where she stood in the center holding Holiday's bridle. I shook my head.

"Sultan," I replied. I saw Amanda with a slight grin on her face watching me atop this huge, prancing black gelding, unsuccessfully trying to get him to walk. "Relax," Sally told me. "Lower your energy and he'll lower his." *Okay, lower your energy.* I concentrated. *Walk. Walk.* I pictured hooves in the rhythmic beat of one, two, three, four.

One, two, three, four. Soon Sultan's hooves were following that same beat. Amanda and Holiday were on the rail now.

"Okay, girls, trot!" Sally called, hands on her hips. All I had to do was stop thinking walk, and we were off. I settled myself into the gait, raised my hands, clucked him up and sent him down the rail. "Good, Maria. Just a touch more collection. Amanda, you need to sit back more and bend your elbows. Let your horse's head come to meet you, not the other way around. There, that's better." I made a quick glance over at Holiday, just to see what he looked like under saddle. In the second I turned my head, Sultan immediately lengthened his stride and we were way too fast coming out of the turn.

"A ha!" Sally exclaimed. "See that? You can't let him get that fast. You just lost all the collection you had. You don't need to be flying. Don't let him get ahead of you like that! You cannot give this horse an inch or he'll take a mile." I nodded and worked him back under my seat. "Okay, girls, down to a walk."

"Whoop, whoop, walk." I sat down deeply in the saddle, lowered my hands, and kept my left leg ready should he decide to spin again. It was his latest trick, to get out of walking, Sally said. Boy, was I glad we weren't required to flat walk in the show ring!

"Canter!" Sally called. I touched Sultan with my leg as I angled him toward the rail, and he sprung into a slow, smooth canter. I sat back, touching the bridle and bringing his every stride back to me. The scent of fall was in the air, and I sat to the beat of his canter, reveling in the joy of riding and the pleasure of being outside on such a day. "Good, Amanda. Now raise your hands a little and bend your elbows. Steady your lower leg. Good, Maria." I glanced over at her. She held her hands up as if she were riding, to demonstrate. "Touch, touch, touch..." she moved her wrists in rhythm with her words. I nodded, repeated it to myself in my head. Touch, touch, touch... "Down to a walk, girls."

Our lesson was soon over and I had untacked Sultan and given him a bath. We were now standing outside, in the shade. I held his lead rope in one hand, an iced tea in the other, waiting for him to cool out. Emily had brought me the tea. Jessica was up riding her young three-gaited As Time Goes By, affectionately known as Timmy. Emily's lesson was next. Angel, her grey park mare, was all tacked and waiting to go. Amanda and Holiday stood a few yards away. "Does he like that?" she motioned at the can I held.

"I don't know, I don't think I ever gave him any," I replied. I poured a little tea into the palm of my hand and offered it to Sultan. He bumped his nose against it, and then greedily licked it up. "Guess he does," I laughed, wiping my hand on my shorts.

"Holiday likes lemonade better," Amanda said, "and pretzels. He'll really eat anything." She took a sip of her own tea. I placed my hand on Sultan's chest to check if he was cooling out all right.

"Nearly cool," I patted his neck. He swished his tail. "So how was your ride?" I asked Amanda. "I didn't really get to see any of it." I thought of the one time I had tried to…I'd paid for that!

"Better than last time. That's all I ask. I think Holiday likes this Saddleseat stuff, but it's really different for me. I keep forgetting one thing or another."

"You'll get it soon," I said encouragingly. I checked Sultan once more, then led him inside. In his stall I cross-tied him as I put my tack away. Then I brushed him off, gave him a peppermint and turned him loose. By then Jess was back with Timmy. I stopped by his stall to ask how it went and pat him on the neck. Then I headed up to watch Emily's ride. She was cantering the first way. "Circle!" Sally called. She was halfway through and I knew she wouldn't make it. Angel's body wasn't bent properly. She was tricky about cantering circles. If her head was bent too far she'd fall out of the canter, which is exactly what she did. Emily set her up again, and was out on the rail. "Again!" Sally called. This time Emily bent the horse's body around her leg and Angel continued cantering. "Perfect. Down to a walk," Sally called.

When Emily's lesson was over, she parked Angel out, dismounted, and rolled up her stirrups. Taking hold of the horse's bridle, she led her over to where I was standing and we headed down. "How was she?" I placed a hand on the mare's sweaty neck.

"Pretty good." Emily led her into her stall, and I handed her the halter as she slid off her bridle. I hung her bridle on her hook on the stall and leaned against the wall.

"She looked good." I rested my head back on the wood. Then I remembered. "Oh, yeah, did you hear about Sally's friend? I think her name was Carol or something with a 'C.' I know her horse's name was Major. She rode huntseat, but he's a Saddlebred. Something happened at some recent show and Carol's in the hospital and Major broke some bone in his leg. Anyway, they might keep him here while he recovers, but don't say anything to anyone because it's not for sure yet." Emily shook her head.

"I won't." She tossed me a leg wrap she'd taken off Angel. Once we'd taken care of Angel I picked her saddle up and motioned for her to get the rest of her tack.

"Let's take this up and I'll show you a picture of Major," I said. We clambered up the stairs to the tack room. I flipped open the photo album all the way to the last page, and once again found myself looking at a breathtaking liver chestnut Saddlebred in huntseat attire. I couldn't take my eyes off him. "Timeless," I said.

"Huh?" Emily asked.

"His name," I explained.

"Oh." She stepped back. "Well, he sure is beautiful." I hung her saddle on her rack and nodded.

"Yeah. I hope his leg heals. I think Sally said it was his coffin bone."

"I'm not exactly sure where that is," Emily said, "but it

doesn't sound good." Shaking my head,
    "No, it certainly doesn't." I walked to the stairs.

Chapter 2

Back at home I sat at the dinner table picking at the spaghetti on my plate. I had eaten a large lunch and wasn't really hungry. "How was Sultan today?" Dad asked.

"Fine," I said. "He didn't want to walk and tried to spin...kind of did this half-rear thing and..."

"He reared?" Dad interrupted. I shook my head and sighed.

"No Dad, he didn't really rear, he just kind of spun. On his back legs."

"Oh." He went back to eating. Jessica's eyes were twinkling at me from across the table. I raised my eyebrows at her, and she got the message. I didn't need Dad thinking Sultan was dangerous or something.

"Guess what?" I said to change the subject mostly. "Sultan and I rode with Amanda, the new rider I was telling you about. She has a Morgan named Holiday. He's really cute. They used to do western."

"That's nice," Dad said placidly. "And how was Timmy?" He turned to Jessica.

"Timmy was very good. I just need to stay ahead of him a little more, and I'd say we're doing really well." Dad nodded.

"That's good." I took a half-hearted bite of spaghetti. As Dad and Jessica talked I felt my mind wander from their conversation to Major. He might be coming to Sunny Ridge. I hoped he did. Then we could help him to get better. But another part of my mind said, What if he didn't? Could I bear that? I decided not to think about that. Major had to get better with our help. When we were through eating I reached for a few of the plates and Jessica reached for some. As we began to carry them toward the sink I turned around hearing a clatter. I saw a broken plate on the floor, and Jessica looking down at it with a shocked expression on her face.

"Did someone just break a plate?" Dad called from the other room.

"I didn't really break one," Jess called back, looking at me. "One just kind of…slipped out of my hand. And shattered."

I had two minutes, I thought as I stared at a picture of Emily and I along with Eric, Tina and the rest of the "barn crew." It was taped to my locker wall. It was Monday morning and I had barely enough time to make it to my first period class. Standing up, the kid with the locker above mine swung his door open. It was perfect timing on both of our parts and it hit my head. "Ouch!" I yelled, raising my hand to my throbbing forehead.

"Oh, did I hit you? I'm so sorry!" He seemed genuinely concerned so I smiled. "Really, I'm sorry. Are you okay?" he turned to his friends beside him. "Oh look, I hit her! Really you're not going to pass out or anything, are you?"

"No, really, I'm okay." Glancing at my watch, "Oh shoot, I've gotta go. Bye!" I swung my bag to my shoulder and raced off, ignoring the school's no running policy. I charged into the classroom and plopped into my seat just as the bell ended. Curious eyes were upon me as class began, and I attempted to catch my breath from my sprint. I didn't care. I had saved myself from a detention.

It was Algebra class and as usual I was lost. I had long ago stopped tormenting myself by trying to understand all of it. Math totally confused me, and sometimes it was just better to let it slide by and accept it without questioning it. I had a creative sort of mind, which oftentimes got me into trouble with subjects such as math or science. I didn't like rules, and always challenged the rules. What made it worse was that much of the time the math didn't even follow its *own* rules, and a list of exceptions compiled quickly in my head. So, I was left struggling in the dark, fighting with numbers and variables and equal signs, trying desperately to make them become what they were supposed to equal, wondering who the heck was ever going to need to use all of this once they graduated. No matter how hard I tried, I always left the Algebra room feeling drained and frustrated.

After Algebra was English class. I liked English mostly, but I couldn't write an essay to save my life. What I thought was my best came back with an 85 on it. Alright, so I wasn't the world's greatest essay writer. I'd improve on the next one. I'd take what I learned in class and use it for my next one…and still get an 85.

Finally lunch arrived. I stood next to the drink machine and watched as it dropped a cute little plastic cup and filled it with the ice and lemonade that I chose. When the "thank you" sign came on, I opened the door and lifted it out. Sitting down with the usual group at lunch, I found my mind wandering to the horses, as usual. Two girls at the end of the table were giggling over some note lying in front of them. I had never figured what was in those notes, and didn't lower myself to beg to find out, as did so many others. Some were e-mails, some hand written, but most were print outs of instant messages sent by boyfriends or crushes the night before. I sighed and went about eating my lunch, holding a casual conversation with Jackie who had a locker next to mine.

"So, are you going to the game?" she asked me. I shrugged.

"I don't know yet. I might." It wasn't really a lie. There was always a possibility that one night I might suddenly feel inclined to go to "the game." True, it was a very slim chance, but it was a chance. Of course, I did not let on that I had absolutely no idea what kind of game it was (football, maybe?) where it was, or who we were playing. "I haven't decided yet."

"Oh well you really should come. *Everyone's* going." *Great,* I thought, *more of a reason not to go.* I hated crowds.

"I'm busy tonight," I lied.

"It's Thursday night," she said. I actually had an excuse then.

"I have a riding lesson Thursday night. I don't think I can make it, but I'll try." *When pigs fly.* I'd never trade a lesson for a football game! Shaking my head, I finished my lunch and prepared for my next class.

Chapter 3

The Past

Carol stood in front of Memphis, one hand on each side of the bridle. "Whoa," she murmured, waiting for Sally to put her left foot in the stirrup of the nervous horse, and mount up. Once she was in the saddle and had gathered her reins, Carol stepped to the side and waited. Memphis was eccentric. He was a skittish animal, and disliked crowds, but could be brilliant when he was on.

"Carol, can you go check the ring and make sure that nothing too odd like aliens or spaceships is in there that will scare this nutcase anymore than usual? I don't feel like falling off in Freedom Hall." Sally clucked to the dark liver chestnut park horse and urged him into a trot to warm up.

"Sure. Don't do anything too dumb until I get back!" Carol warned the 3 year old gelding. She liked Memphis, despite his quirks, and had spent a good deal of time with him over the summer, filling in as assistant trainer for her friend Sally, until a new one could be found. She planned on getting back into more serious showing herself, as soon as she found the horse. Her husband, Jeff, wouldn't be too thrilled…but he'd get over it, she grinned.

She showed her pass to the guard, and moved in along the white rail of the showring, and spent a minute or two scanning the arena for anything that might spook the flighty Memphis. The crowd alone might do him in, she thought. At the moment, a class of weanlings was in the ring. Carol dropped her eyes to the youngsters and froze.

There in front of her was a gorgeous liver chestnut colt. His handlers seemed delighted to let him show off, the header just held the lead at the end of the leather, and let the colt trot. The tailer shook his bag once, and it was all that the colt needed. Carol knew she should return to Sally and Memphis, but she couldn't leave. Not yet. Two more babies trotted in, and after what seemed like an eternity, the winner was called. Then second place…the liver chestnut. His name was Timeless, but you could barely hear it above the deafening roar from the crowd. The judges had made their choice, but as it happens occasionally in Freedom Hall, when a great one comes along, the crowd had chosen differently, and they had chosen him. Carol was already heading for the in-gate, thoughts of Memphis and aliens already long gone from her mind. They would all want him…but she was getting there first. He was her chance, the one she'd been waiting for. No matter what she had to do, that colt was coming home with her.

Thursday when I arrived at the barn (not the football game) I heard that Major had also arrived. I strolled down the aisle to see him. He was at the far end of the aisle, away from the hustle and bustle of all the other horses being worked or tacked. There was a difference in him from the photos I'd seen. There was no spark in his eyes, no interested expression with ears forward. He didn't hold himself proudly; his head was drooping down as he stood at the back of his stall. There was no bravado or audacity when I clucked, though he finally lifted his head to glance at me. He looked at me for a moment, and then turned away. I called his name and he raised his head half an inch, then thought better of it and lowered it again. I wanted to go visit with him in his stall but didn't. I had to go tack Sultan.

As I cross-tied him, I paid attention to his eyes, burning with interest and full of excitement, eager for a ride. As I threw the saddle up and settled it on his back, I thought that healing Major might be harder than I'd imagined, and that the leg might be the easiest thing to heal. Veterinarians could help the leg, but what could you do about a broken spirit?

Sultan and I were walking slowly around the outdoor ring. Sally was on the phone. After a long time, Sally's mother came up and told me to just start riding; Sally would be a while. So we picked up the trot. We were cantering the second direction when Sally entered the ring. She didn't look happy. Her hand on her forehead, she sighed. "I'm sorry I took so long, Maria," she said as I brought Sultan into the middle. "That was Jeff again…Carol wants to come out of the hospital, but they want to keep her there at least the rest of the week…she wants to see Major. I don't think she should, not yet. She says she might want to put him down if the leg is that bad…but don't worry," she glanced at my face. "She just came to, she's not thinking straight. The leg will mend in time, if he has the chance. And he'll have the chance if I have anything to say about it." I was stroking Sultan's neck; I didn't know what to say. I nodded.

"Well," she motioned with her hand, "go out on the rail and let me see one last trot."

Leading Sultan down to his stall, I watched his eyes sparkle and ears prick toward every sound. That was what Major was missing. I wasn't sure if it was something that, once lost, could be regained. Even if his leg healed, he wouldn't be the same, and if he didn't care, if he didn't fight…his leg might not heal. We had to make him fight. But the problem was we couldn't make him, we had to make him want to.

For awhile there wasn't much we could do with Major but try and stop by his stall to cheer him up. Before and after lessons, in any free moment we had, we'd head down to his stall. He rarely seemed happy to see us, but I think he was glad we came. One particular time as I stood outside his stall after a Thursday afternoon lesson, I felt a hand on my shoulder. "You want to help him, don't you?" Sally asked me, her eyes searching mine. I nodded.

"Yeah." We stood in silence for a moment. I heard her sigh behind me. "You think he'll heal?" I asked.

"You don't mean the leg." It was a statement. "The leg will heal all right." She shook her head. "Boy, he was something. He was a fighter. Physically I think he'll be fine." She looked me in the eye. "But you know that." I looked away, toward the horse. "This'll be a tough one, kid. I'm going to try, for Carol, and for him. The thing is, Maria, he was always a very proud animal. Look at him: he thinks he's defeated, he thinks it's over. We've got to show him that it's not." I nodded, watching the horse's ear flick back for a moment.

"That's hard."

"That's very hard," she clarified. I paused, thinking for a moment.

"How's Carol?"

"She blames herself for what happened. She's out of the hospital, and is heading up to see him tonight. I guess she'll decide then if she wants to put him down or not. But don't worry too much on that—I can at least convince her to put it off 'til later—once she's had time to think. And believe me, once she's had time to think she'll give him the chance to heal." I nodded.

"Oh."

"Of course, it wasn't anyone's fault. But she said she should've quit after his first two seasons like she planned originally. But he loved to jump! That's why she returned to it in the first place. You don't stop a horse from doing what they love to do! He was spectacular, and they swept away everyone on their circuit. He was a good ambassador for the Saddlebred, all right." She paused. "It was never his motion or headset that set him apart when he was shown at Louisville as a youngster, it was the way he carried himself that drew everyone's eyes to him. That's what we've gotta get back. Think you can?"

"Me?" the surprise rang in my voice. How was this turning into a Maria project? She patted my arm with a soft smile, turned and walked away down the aisle, leaving me to my thoughts.

Chapter 4

I was on the internet that night doing research for a school project. My mind kept drifting, so finally I logged off and headed to my room to think. *Why had I chosen to get involved with this?* I wondered. I had a history with these sorts of things, but I realized that I hadn't really chosen. Like so many things in my life, it had simply happened. Emily and I would have never become friends, had Angel not turned up missing that rainy day years ago. My dad would have never bought Sultan for me; he would've been shipped off to some other barn, far away, never to be seen at Sunny Ridge again. And had Night Watch not been stolen and passing as "Victory March," our beloved champion, Timmy, would not even exist. Jessica and I would have never gotten along. I was the one that figured out the truth about Night Watch, I helped convince Emily's parents to purchase Triumph, and I played a leading roll in turning her into one of the best harness ponies on our show circuit.

Now, another adventure and challenge stood before me. Getting involved though, always opens the door to possible hurt. What if Sally could not convince Carol, and Major was put down now? Right away? Tomorrow? Could I bear that?

I didn't even know Carol. I was assuming she was a reasonable and good person because she was Sally's friend, and I had trouble picturing Sally befriending someone too different from herself. But then I thought of my own friends. With some of them, I had very little in common. Even Emily and I had some very large distinctions and dissenting points of view. But Carol? I knew nothing about her, save she was a friend of Sally's. I could only hope that stood for something.

Even if she gave him the chance it would be a long road. I could see it now: vet upon vet, taking stock in Bute, midnight phone calls, all of the set backs…The vet had ordered at least six months of stall rest for him. That was a ridiculously long time for a horse to be cooped up, but it was the time needed to mend his leg. Six months was the minimum, depending on how well the healing progressed. Eventually, though, he would have to be hand walked, or he would lose a lot of his muscle tone from just standing around. The whole process could take up to 12 months. That was a long time. Twelve months would end next September. When school began. When summer ended. I wondered what Carol thought when she saw Major. Had she made her decision? I didn't understand how she could blame herself, but then again I'd never been through an accident like that. If she had decided to try healing the leg, I didn't understand why Major was still here, since she was out of the hospital now. Perhaps it was because she needed to heal herself before she could help him. Sally knew this, I reasoned, because she was her friend, but mostly because she was Sally.

✦

Major. That's what Carol called him. He had grown a lot since she'd purchased him, and had now matured into an elegant 3 year old. Sally came over to Carol's once or twice a week to visit her friend and check on Major's progress. "It's good to see a young horse here again," Sally smiled, scratching Major's neck.

"Yeah, for a while the old boys were the only residents." Carol laughed, glancing over at her retired jumpers from her younger years. "Major here has so much energy. You should see the disgusted looks they give him!" Carol was playing with Major's tongue and the horse was tilting his head sideways and wiggling it back and forth. "You're silly," Carol shook her head. "Shall we tack you up so that Sally can see your progress?" The gelding bobbed his head, as if in agreement, and both ladies laughed.

Carol had been the first one on his back, but Sally mounted today, and took him for a spin around the ring. "For a 3 year old, he's very smooth and responsive, and his canter is to die for!" Sally said to Carol, with a touch of amazement.

"Isn't he great?" Carol looked at Major with pride. "He's so smart, training him is easy!"

"Yeah," Sally smiled, dismounting and giving the horse a hearty pat, "the good ones are like that."

My book bag weighed like lead on my way home from school on Friday. "I think I'm bringing every book I own home tonight," I grunted to Jackie as I slammed my locker shut and she hers.

"Me too, and it's Friday! Don't they know there's not supposed to be homework on the weekend?" she asked.

"Yeah, I mean, some of us have lives," I laughed. I swung my book bag to my shoulder. "See ya, Jackie." I bounded down the steps and out the door, sped toward the bus and hopped in. We were soon roaring away from school and toward home. I opened my bag and began my weekend work. There was no way I was doing it Saturday. Saturdays were for one thing only—riding. I worked until the stop before mine, and then began packing it all away. "Bye!" I called to the bus driver, as I sprang out of my seat and down the stairs. I raced up our front stairs and reached for the door handle. It was opened from the inside by Jessica. Dad wasn't home yet; he'd made some stop along the way.

"Lots of work?" Jess looked at my bag.

"As usual," I tossed it on the couch and went to get myself a snack.

"Well, get it done tonight if you can," Jess suggested sympathetically.

"I'm trying," I went back to work. When Dad got home I was on Biology. By suppertime I was into World Studies.

Dinner was a quiet affair. I was tired, Dad was tired, and Jess was tired. We had macaroni and cheese which is what we make when we're tired. Easy to make, easy to clean up. There wasn't much talk, and once I was through eating I excused myself to go and work some more. I still had to read and answer questions in English, do a worksheet, and define all the words in the first two sections of the chapter for Algebra, and write down all my information on what I planned to do for my history project.

Chapter 5

It had taken all night, but I'd gotten all my work done except for studying for my two tests, which I would do on Sunday. Come Saturday Jess drove me to the barn, as usual. I got out and headed inside. Emily was just arriving then, too. "Hey, Em!" I called, waving. She ran to catch up. "So what's new?"

"Not much. I have so much work this year though," she groaned.

"Yeah, me too. You should've seen my book bag last night." That ended the school talk. We were free for now, and would make the most of it. I cross-tied Sultan and groomed him, wrapped his legs and strapped on the splint boots. Emily had gotten my saddle and other tack, so I swung the saddle over the pad on his back and set about attaching and tightening the girth. I ducked under the cross-tie on Sultan's left side and pulled with all my might. "C'mon Sultan, quit holding your breath!" I waited a moment, and tried again. This time I got it another hole tighter. I patiently bridled him, and we started up to the ring. As I unrolled my stirrups and hooked up my draw reins, Sally walked up beside me leading a younger girl behind her.

"Maria, this is Tara. She's come to visit the stable today and see what it's like, so she can decide if she wants to take lessons here. She's going to watch your lesson today." I nodded.

"Hi, Tara."

"Hi," she smiled shyly. I glanced at Sally who gave me a wink and leg-up into the saddle.

"She's still undecided. The vet's coming today," she whispered before I asked Sultan to walk off. I knew she was speaking of Carol and Major and I felt a greater weight descend on my heart. I knew that concentrating on riding Sultan was not going to happen this lesson.

Sally seemed tired today. She called instructions from the center of the ring, occasionally explaining things to Tara or her mother. Sultan was fairly well-behaved, and I was grateful for that. At least we'd given Tara's mother a good first impression, with none of Sultan's usual 'didoes.' Sally sent the girl down to the barn with me afterwards as she spoke with her mother. "So, how old are you?" I asked her.

"Eight," she answered from Sultan's doorway.

"Do you ride now?" I asked.

"Not really." She paused, "But I really want to though. My mom rode when she was young."

"Ah" I nodded, slipping the bridle off and exchanging it for the halter. I pulled the saddle, took off his leg gear, and handed her a leg wrap. "Wanna learn how to roll it up?" She nodded. So I showed her. "You put the strip like this…" I held mine out and inspected hers. "Good, now you begin to roll in, like this…" Once she had finished, she asked,

"Why do you do that?"

"So next time someone wants to use it to protect their horse's legs it's all ready for them to roll right on." She helped me put my gear away and cool Sultan out. While he was still cross-tied I took her on a tour of the barn. "Here is Milo, Lilac, Penny, and Wind Song. This is Champ, Melody,

Pepper, Cal, and Irish. Over here is Dawn. This is Triumph, the black one here, and next to her is Simba." The ponies intrigued the girl.

"What do they do?" she asked, peering into Simba's stall.

"Well, he is what we call a roadster pony. He pulls a little two-wheeled cart and trots really fast. That black one there, Triumph, is a harness pony and pulls a viceroy, a smaller four wheeled cart." She reached her hand up to pat Simba on the nose. We finished our tour. "Who's that?" she asked as we headed back up the aisle, pointing at the only stall I hadn't mentioned.

"That's Major," I said, carefully choosing my words. "He hurt his leg and is staying here until…until he gets better."

"Oh. Can I see him?" she asked, rushing toward his door. She peered in. "Does it hurt an awful lot?" I had no idea what in the world to say to her, but I knew I couldn't tell her the truth, that the vet was coming today, and what he said would decide the horse's fate.

"Oh, he's doing all right," I said, not even sure if my words were true or not. I guided her back up the aisle. "Let's go see if Sultan can be turned loose."

"Turned loose?" she asked, as we continued toward his stall, her stride matching mine.

"Taken off the cross-ties," I clarified. "See a horse can get sick if they drink too much cold water when they're hot from a hard work out. So to prevent that we leave them on these things," I motioned to the cross-ties as I unclipped them from Sultan's halter. "so they can't reach their water until they're cooled out. That way they don't get sick." I slipped his halter off and gave him a pat on the neck. She patted his nose. Sultan snorted and turned away. I closed the door.

"He's drinking now!" she exclaimed.

"Yep, he's cool now, it's okay. And watch, he'll only take one or two gulps and then be done." True to my words, he finished up and began searching the floor of his stall for what hay he had left from breakfast. "Come on," I motioned to

Tara. "Let's go find your mother." She followed me out to the ring where Jess and Timmy were finishing up and Angel and Emily were circling the first way of the ring at a walk. "There you are Tara," her mother exclaimed. "Did you see the barn?" The girl nodded. "I'm sorry, your name is…?" she looked at me.

"Maria," I smiled.

"Well thanks for showing Tara around. She's really excited about learning to ride. I've told her a lot of stories about when I was a kid and did a lot of riding."

"I can see she is," I said. "Well, see you later!" I waved and headed back down to the barn. Jess was bringing Timmy down as well, and as she led him through the aisle, she told me she was going to be leaving as soon as she was finished with him, and she'd be back to pick me up later, around 1:30 or 2:00. I told her that would be fine. I did a few things that needed to be done, and leaning on the fence, I talked with Eric while we watched Emily finish up her lesson on Angel. Emily and I cooled Angel out, did a few other jobs, and went up the stairs in the barn to eat lunch. I settled myself between Emily and Eric and across from Holly. Amanda was also seated at the table. She was riding during Eric's normal lesson today, until Sally came up with a spot of her own for her. We laughed and talked as we ate lunch, discussing everything from our lessons that day, to upcoming shows. Every time I'd smile, I'd think of Major and it would quickly fade away. It didn't seem fair that we were enjoying life when his might soon be over.

Eric stood up halfway through, gathered the remnants of his lunch and pushed his hand through his hair. "I guess I'll start to tack up Irish," He made a toss of his aluminum foil that had covered his sandwich at the trash and made it. He headed down. Emily and I finished up and strolled down the stairs as well. I started in the direction of Irish's stall where I found the gelding cross-tied and being tacked by Eric. He was just putting on the first leg wrap when I arrived. When he finished, I tossed him the other from the floor outside the stall. "Catch!" I threw. He snatched it from the air as Irish snorted with large eyes.

"You scared the poor horse," Emily held out a hand and patted the liver chestnut on the neck.

"Yeah, I can see he's just terrified." I tossed Eric both splint boots. "You're riding with Amanda," I said. "That's one cute Morgan she's got."

"Oh, I know! You should have seen him the other day when Sally worked him." He straightened up, ducked the cross-tie and got his saddle and pad. Irish flattened his ears to his neck and snapped at the air. He swished his tail as Eric adjusted the pad and laid the saddle over it. He began biting the cross-tie when the girth was tightened. "There, I'm done." He patted the horse's shoulder and Irish's ears immediately came forward. Reaching for the bridle, he undid the cross-ties and slid off the halter which I stepped forward to take from him. I hung it on the door. Eric buckled the cavesson and throatlatch, attached the draw-reins and clucked once, leading him out. Emily and I followed behind down the aisle into the sunlight, and up to the ring. Emily was telling me a story about her lab partner at school when Sally called to us. "Girls, if you see the vet pull up in the truck, call me, okay?" We nodded. From where we stood outside the ring we had a clear view of the driveway. I set my foot on the lowest rung of the fence.

"Must be for Major." Emily glanced at me. I nodded mutely and she continued with her story. Eric on Irish and Amanda aboard Holiday were now walking on the rail the first direction.

"Trot!" Sally's voice seemed to come from a distance as I listened half-heartedly to Emily's story. As the hoof beats of the horses drew nearer, I automatically pulled back from the rail as they passed. "Okay Eric, he's warmed up now, start pressing him! Amanda you need a line from your shoulder to your hip to your heel. I want you to look down at your legs…yeah, look down. There. Where's your line? You need to pull that leg back and get it in place." When the horses came down to a walk and were about to go into a canter, that's when I saw the truck. It crawled slowly up the driveway and parked among the other cars. My stomach lurched. I knew that truck.

"Sally!" I called. She swung around.

"Okay, I'm coming. Stay up here," she said to me, "and keep an eye on Amanda for me. I won't be long." I nodded, and ducked under the fence and into the ring. The horses were still cantering. Eric was doing fine with Irish, and Amanda was doing well, too. She was a good rider; she just needed to learn proper Saddleseat form. They kept cantering, and I was about to tell them to stop when Eric finally glanced at me, and seeing Sally was nowhere around, said, "Whoop, whoop, walk," and brought the horse down. Amanda followed suit. Eric gave the gelding a pat on the neck, and after walking halfway around the ring, swung him toward the rail in a reverse. Amanda turned Holiday and both of them picked up the trot. Emily got out some of the "toys" used to excite the horses and started banging away. It seemed to me they were doing fine on their own, which was just as well, because my mind was elsewhere. "Legs," I reminded Amanda once. When they were about done trotting, Sally returned. I nervously glanced toward her, dreading her words, but wishing she'd hurry up and say them.

"He said the leg is a little worse than they thought at first," she told me. The breath caught in my throat and I felt sick.

"So…?" I asked timidly.

"So now I have to talk to Carol and tell her, and see what she wants to do." She replied. I was scared for Major, but I was a little angry, too. It somehow didn't seem fair that someone so out of it, uninvolved, should get to decide the fate of this horse. I mean, she'd been to see him only once since he'd been here. As if reading my mind Sally said, "It's a good thing that she hasn't been to see him except for that first time. He seems so downcast that it makes the injury look ten times worse. And he doesn't seem to have improved either, since she was here the last time. Believe it or not, Maria, this is a tough decision, even for me. The extent of this injury is phenomenal. The only reason I'm lobbying for a chance at recovery is because I just have this gut feeling that he's a horse that can make it." She paused, and when I remained silent, asked, "How are they doing?" and motioned toward the riders.

"Good." I normally would've said more, but not today. Normally I would've pointed out how Irish's transitions down were choppy; how Amanda needed work on her diagonals…Sally's eyes flickered back to my face.

"Good," she said. "That's good." She turned toward the riders on the rail, watching them. "The vet said recovery is possible, but some horses just can't put up with it. He said if I know the horse that well, and he has the fight in him I say he does, then he'd give it a chance. If Carol decides to give Major that chance, the vet says after the six months we can—and should—start taking him on short walks so he doesn't lose all his muscle tone just standing around." I nodded.

"Okay."

"We just have to be very careful to keep him quiet so he doesn't do that leg anymore damage." I nodded again, still waiting. "More horse Eric! You and Emily can be in charge of that." She said it without taking her eyes off the others. I nodded a third time, and turned to go. She said nothing so I took one step then another… "Then we can start turning him out in the paddock."

If we even get that far, I thought, but I said, "Okay" and ducked back under the fence next to Emily, to report what Sally had said. Emily drummed her fingers on the fence. I bent down to pick up Tabby, the orange barn cat, who had been methodically rubbing against my legs. I cuddled him against me and he purred louder. Eric and Amanda finally lined up in the center of the ring and dismounted. The day continued.

That night was torture. Sally was supposed to visit Carol that afternoon, and she had promised to call me afterwards, either way. It was 6:30 now, and I was sitting by the phone, only half watching the movie on TV.

"Maria, do you want some popcorn?" Dad called.

"No, thanks," I replied stiffly.

By quarter of seven, I could've cried. What was taking so long? Was she still at Carol's? Were they arguing over Major's chances? Or…had Sally just forgotten to call me? I decided that must be the case, and I had just entered my room to dig her number out of my address book when our phone rang. "I'll get it!" I launched myself down the stairs and snatched it off the cradle, pressing the "mute" button on the television remote control at the same time.

"Maria?"

"Yeah, it's me." I swallowed. "What's up?"

"Well, it wasn't easy, but I convinced her to at least wait a bit and see if he begins to improve. So for now, Major's still with us."

Chapter 6

It had been a warm day near the end of March that Carol witnessed one of the greatest feats a horse had ever performed, and knew in that moment that Major's destiny was decided for him.

He had been turned out in the large pasture behind the barn, because it was such a pleasant spring day. He had trotted around a few times, and then settled down to cropping grass, and Carol continued with her barn work of cleaning stalls and tidying up. The horses were always turned out one by one, when their stalls were being cleaned, but Carol thought they would enjoy extra turn-out time that day. Her breeding stallion had just been sold, so she decided to turn Comet out in his now empty pasture and put it to good use. The two pastures were next to each other, but not adjacent. A few feet separated the fences, and the stallion enclosure boasted an extra high fence to prevent him from escaping.

She was just leading Comet through the gate when Major noticed them from across the pasture. As she turned the elderly horse loose, she watched Major come barreling toward them. "Easy, buddy," she thought, "you're going to have trouble stopping when you get to that fence." Comet had been munching on grass, but his head came up when he noticed the youngster racing his way. As he approached, it became apparent to Carol that he had *no intentions of stopping. What should she do? Her brain was frantic, but she was out of time. He approached his pasture fence, lifted off in a graceful arc, clearing it by feet, which was a good thing because he was still soaring across the space separating the two pastures, and over the stallion's fence. He landed without touching the top rail. Carol's jaw dropped.*

✦

It was a warm day for December and we were on Christmas break. We had ridden together—me, Emily, Eric, Tina, Christine, Amanda, Tara, Sam and Claire, another young rider like Tara, except Claire had been riding Saddleseat her whole life. We rode in two groups, and afterwards hung out together. Claire and Tara were already good friends, and at the moment they were chasing each other with lunge whips from the outdoor ring. The rest of us were sitting on the concrete outside the barn talking and snacking on potato chips. It was sunny enough to shed our jackets, and we had. Every now and then a scream pierced the air, but other than that it was quite peaceful. "They're gonna fall," Eric commented.

"So go get them." Tina grabbed some more chips. No one moved.

"Falling never hurt anyone." I smushed a couple of our jackets into a pillow and laid down with my head on them. I continued eating the potato chips. No one told me I was going to choke, like my dad would have. I was grateful. The two girls ran up to us and sat down, breathing hard, but happy and not worn out in the least. They began eating the chips. Claire laid down like I was and continued eating them. I didn't tell her she was going to choke. She didn't.

It was three months since Major's accident, and half-way

through his stall rest period. I thought about this as I lay there, not choking on my chips. Another three months, and if the vets okayed it, we would begin hand-walking him. Carol hadn't been to see Major since that first visit, as far as I knew, but I knew that Sally had been to see Carol many times. Eric now held the chip bag upside down. "No more," he scrunched it up and got to his feet to throw it out. Tara got up and went after him with a lunge whip, so he took it from her and threw her over his shoulder, and left her struggling there.

"So, what's everybody wearing to the banquet this year?" I questioned, while I had them all together. I was referring to the yearly end-of-season banquet where your points are added up and you or your horse receives an award for your performance that year.

"I'm wearing a black dress," Tina volunteered.

"I'm wearing this…well, it's hard to describe…it's a dress, but it's not a dress, it's like…" Christine attempted to explain.

"Oh, that's nice Christine," I laughed. "It's a dress but it's not a dress. Where'd you get it? I want one!"

"Yeah," Amanda chimed in, "me too!"

"You know what I mean!" she exclaimed.

"No, actually we don't." I chuckled.

"Well, you'll see it at the banquet."

"Now I can't wait. I've got to see this dress." Emily grinned.

"I can't wait either." Sam got up.

"Yeah," I groaned, "because you win all of the door prizes."

"Yep! Well, I'm out of here, gang. See you all!"

"Bye, Sam!" we all called. He had his driver's license, and could leave whenever he was ready. Everyone else had to wait for a ride, but I never minded. Giggles were heard coming from the outdoor ring, and in a few minutes Tara and Claire were prancing about the barn pretending to be horses; five-gaited Saddlebreds at that. That's when the barn door opened. It was Sally.

"Is there a party going on here or something I wasn't invited to?"

"You're invited now," I assured her, "Sit down." She did sit.

"Yeah, Sally," Tina exclaimed, "Christine's wearing a dress to the banquet, but it's not a dress."

"Oh, that ought to be interesting," Sally laughed. "So what are you kids doing now? You want to help me plant some bulbs?"

"Isn't it a little late for planting bulbs?" I asked, sitting up and separating the coats.

"Yeah, but this is the only time I get to do it."

"Hey, whatever works." I stood up and stretched. In a moment we were all on our feet, walking toward the shed where Sally kept the lawn care equipment such as the riding mower. She gathered some spades and the bulbs, and we all grabbed a box. Sally led the way to the flower beds around the barn, and starting on the right side, we began to plant. Christine read the back of the package of bulbs and told us how deep to plant them. I dug and Emily placed a bulb in and covered it up. Amanda, Tina and Eric did the same, starting at the other end. Claire and Tara were now playing with Snickers, the farm dog. Claire came and sat down next to me after a few minutes. "Can I help?" she asked, picking a bag of bulbs out of the cardboard box.

"Sure you can," I answered her. "You can open that up and hold it for Emily. If Tara wants to help, she can do the same for the others."

"Okay." It didn't take us long to finish up. We moved onto the other side of the barn, and then planted a few around the back and certain spots around the outdoor ring. Eric and Emily's parents had both arrived by then, and Tara's a few minutes later. Eventually the others filtered out, leaving just Claire and I alone. I had known Jess would be late picking me up and had planned to take Sultan for a walk. I went down to get him, and Claire followed. As I slipped his halter on I asked, "So when's your mom coming?"

"In a half-hour. I asked her to come later." I nodded at this.

"How come?" I knew very well 'how come.'

"I like being here for long times." She scratched Sultan on the neck, and walked along as I let him crop what little brown grass there was, and stop to look, ears forward, eyes focused, at every little sound or movement.

"How long have you been riding?" I asked the girl, curiously. It was the first time I'd ever talked to her alone before.

"Forever," she cupped her hands and let Sultan drop his big black head and sniff them. "How about you?"

"Same here," I answered, leading Sultan forward again. I couldn't remember ever not riding.

"I'd like to ride him," she said quite out of the blue.

"I bet you could." I clucked to Sultan and we headed down to the barn. "Maybe one day you will." I pictured her, so tiny, aboard my big, black three-gaited. I shrugged. She probably could ride him. Nothing surprised me anymore. I stopped by Major's stall before Jessica came. He looked at me, but that was all. "Hey, boy." I put my hand on the stall bars. "How are you?" He didn't come forward.

"Hi, Major!" Claire stood on her tip-toes and looked in. "Come here." The big horse actually raised his head, and his ears came forward. He took a small step toward us.

"We'll see you later, boy." I smiled. He seemed to be making some progress. I just hoped Carol could see it, too. "Small steps are better than none." I turned away.

"Or going backwards!" Claire spun around and bounded down the aisle ahead of me. She didn't know how true that was.

Jess arrived soon after. "So how was Sultan?"

"Good," I climbed in the passenger's seat. "We all rode together."

"How was Major?"

"Well, he's not much different yet."

"All healing takes time." Jess steered the car down the driveway and onto the road. I nodded.

"I know," I said to myself out loud. "I'm trying to be patient...but it's so hard to watch him like that."

✦

Sultan pranced in the center of the indoor arena as Claire sent Sly, a recently acquired, ornery lesson horse, down the straight-away. Still on Christmas break, all my friends and I were taking lessons in pairs. Half-way around the turn Sly broke into a canter and then began racking. "Whoop, trot!" Claire tried to steady him.

"Lighten up!" Sally called. "Trot now!" Sly was a former five-gaited, now 16 and he hated being "humbled" into a pleasure horse. Claire had her hands full trying to convince him that it was time to trot, not rack. Eventually he trotted again, full speed down the rail. "Walk!" Sally called, and then added, "Maria, back on the rail." Sultan wheeled gracefully around when I asked him to turn, and pranced forward, jog-walking along. "What was that?" Sally asked. "Kick him with your left leg! Don't let him do that!" He was, indeed, jogging crookedly again, head toward the rail. Touching the left rein and using my left leg seemed to work....for now. "Claire, into the center. Maria, pick up a canter." We had a nice transition, and he cantered smoothly and slowly. "Walk and reverse. Claire back out on the rail." Sally directed. Once reversed, Sultan didn't want to walk. He tried his spinning off the rail move again. "Nail him, now!" Sally yelled. I gave him a firm whack with my crop and a kick with my right leg. That produced a buck, which got me somewhat forward on his neck. "Seat down!" Sally called. Then she walked out to the center of the ring and walked alongside as Sultan pranced along. His eyes flicked back to her. "Yeah, it's me, Sultan," she said. Then to me, "You need to think ahead of him more. When he tries that, nail him, but he shouldn't be trying it. Get inside his head and know what he's going to do before he does it! Feel it and stop it before it happens."

She walked away a few feet and picked up one of her "toys," this time a milk jug with stones inside it. She got aside of him again and began shaking it. Sultan's neck came back; I shortened my reins and sat down. "Hold him," she said, "Hold him right there. Touch the bridle, sit deep. Hold him! Alright, now trot!" I began posting and lightened up a bit. It was all Sultan needed. Sly and Claire were trotting again as well and we were coming up on them, so I steered Sultan around their right to pass. Sly's ears flicked back, but Sultan's came forward. He loved passing horses. By the time Sultan and I were cantering, the next two riders were arriving. Amanda, Holiday, Tina and Wind Song stood in the center of the arena, the two riders preparing to mount as Claire made the jump down from Sly. "Alright, Maria, you're done," Sally called. I slowed Sultan to a walk and then halted him to dismount as well. After rolling up my stirrups and giving him a pat on the neck, I led him down the aisle to his stall to un-tack.

Claire followed with Sly. I spent a while grooming Sultan, and then returned all my tack to its proper spots. Claire was still in fussing with Sly. The big chestnut gelding let her, but did not seem overly excited about all the currying and petting and hugging. I smiled. Maybe he'd grow to like it. Returning to Sultan's stall I scratched his neck, watching his ears perk forward, and turn his head slightly to the right. When I stopped he gave me a "What happened?" look. I grinned and gave him a final pat before closing his door. "Hang out for a few minutes, then I'll un-crosstie you," I told him. As I walked away I glanced back to see him still standing with his head up and ears forward, eyes bright and alert.

I headed for Major's stall, but someone had beaten me to it. Claire was already there. "What's wrong with him?" she glanced at me.

"Well," I began, "he broke his coffin bone in his left front leg." Oblique Articular fracture. The words echoed in my head.

"How?" Claire asked, looking in at Major once more.

"He was jumping, and when he landed, he twisted his leg…" I cringed at the thought, "and well, that's how it happened."

"Oh." She looked up from his stall. "Well, when's he gonna be better?" I paused.

"Well…it can take up to a year until he can be ridden again."

"A whole year?" she repeated, incredulously. I then remembered how long a year seemed when I was her age. It had seemed like a lifetime.

"Yeah," I said, "a whole year."

✦

"Watch it!" Emily grabbed the handle on the car door. "You almost took out that Toyota!" I was hanging on in the backseat as Emily yelled in the passenger's seat. Anne was at the wheel.

"I did not, Emily, quit exaggerating. I saw her pulling out."

"Oh, yeah, that's why you pressed the gas," she said, not trying to hide the sarcasm in her voice at all. Anne wasn't really that close to the Toyota, but she was driving a little fast for my taste. I gripped the door handle a little tighter. Emily and I had been riding and Anne had driven Triumph. She was now driving us home. *If we make it home, I thought.*

It was our last day of Christmas break, and I dreaded going back to school the next day. I had so much fun on vacation, and Sultan and I had made a lot of progress with my being able to ride him almost every day. "Anyone want to stop for a back-to-school treat?" Anne pointed at a drive-through.

"Can you make it in the parking lot without killing anyone?" Emily growled. Anne just glared at her and smiled at me in the rear-view mirror.

"Ice cream?" she asked.

"Mint chocolate chip." I pictured myself licking a big, tall cone...then I pictured Anne pressing the throttle and the big, tall cone making a big splat on my lap. "In a dish, please," I added.

Chapter 7

Major was good. It hadn't taken Carol long to figure that out. Even Sally was amazed when she'd told her. She got him into huntseat tack, and started preparing him for jumping. They started with cavaletti, and worked up to low cross-rails. The gelding took it all in stride, as if he'd been preparing for this all his life, and perhaps he had. In no time at all, Major was jumping as high as Carol had ever in her life, dared to jump. No matter what she put in front of him, he never refused. She felt that with a horse like Major, she could literally go on to new heights. With him, she'd dare to try anything.

She started competing with him, and he never lost. The competition grumbled at first. What was a Saddlebred doing in the show jumping circuit? They were only meant for Saddleseat! The Saddleseat world grumbled, too. What a waste of a great saddle horse! But once Major continuously out-jumped the others, won blue after blue, took home trophies, and generally amazed millions, the horse papers and magazines started calling him "Super Horse." Every time someone set a limit in front of him, he proved them wrong. Every time someone shoved a record in his path, he broke it. He was a marvel, destined to live forever among the ranks of the truly great equines of the past, the ones whose potential was virtually limitless.

It was Monday morning. I was in a rush to get to Algebra again. "Jackie," I said to my friend whose head was buried inside her locker at the moment, "is it just me or does this day stink already?"

"Mhmp mumph."

"Yeah, exactly. Well, I'll catch you later, I've gotta run." And run I did, and slid into my desk just as the bell rang. My teacher had quit giving me curious looks; he just pretended not to notice. But today we had a substitute. I looked away. Steadying my breathing, I opened my books. We were supposed to be working on page 123. With forty problems to do, I got right down to work. I rested my head on my hand and started writing, but there were too many variables, and my head started throbbing. I turned it sideways to think. Bad move.

"Do you have a problem, er...Maria?" the substitute asked, glancing at the seating chart.

"Er...no. Well, yeah, my head hurts."

"Do you want to go to the nurse?" he asked patiently.

"No thanks. I'll be okay," I answered. I continued, but I really didn't care what X was, and I really didn't care for the process of going about finding it.

I was relieved when it was finally lunchtime. Lunchtime meant food. Lunchtime meant no Algebra, and lunchtime meant sitting with my friends and talking about...stuff. There's no other word for it. That's what we talked about. Just stuff.

"So, how was Algebra?" Jackie asked me. She knew how much I loved math.

"Don't ask," I said darkly. "We had a sub and a lot of

work."

"Yeah, well, be prepared for a pop-quiz on that book we were supposed to read over break," Jackie warned me. We had the same teacher for English class, but she had her earlier in the day. Panic swept through my body.

"Book?" I questioned, probably sounding like a doofus. Then I remembered. I'd read it. I'd read it as quickly as I could in the first few days of vacation. What was it about again? I took a bite of pizza and tried to remember. I had just recalled the character's names when Jackie stood up.

"Come with me to get a soda," she said. I shrugged.

"Okay." It would always remain a mystery to me as to why people could never go by themselves to get a soda, or anything else for that matter. I guess walking alone just didn't look cool. So, I walked with her across the noisy lunch room to the soda machine and she dropped in her money and received a bottle of Coke. Sitting back down, Ashley tapped me on the shoulder.

"Do you have any change I could borrow?" she asked. I dug around in my book bag pocket and produced a quarter and a nickel. Jackie tossed her a dime. "Thanks!" It seemed to me that no one ever had enough money at school for what they wanted to eat. Everyone was always begging, thanking, and borrowing money. *It all probably evens out in the end though*, I thought.

I glanced over at Ashley, furiously flipping through her notebook with a bright yellow highlighter in her hand. She was expertly moving the highlighter along the lines, back and forth, back and forth. I glanced at Jackie, who raised her eyebrows. "I guess she never heard of only highlighting the important notes," Jackie said. Ashley didn't notice.

"What are you doing?" I called across the table. Ashley waved her hand impatiently, not letting her eyes leave the book.

"What?" she asked absently. (She reminded me of the guy behind the lunch counter. It is always so loud, and he can never hear me or get my order straight, or maybe he just has a short attention span. "I'll have a hamburger please."

"A what?"

"A hamburger."

"A what?"

"One hamburger!"

"Two hamburgers?" He holds up two fingers.

"No, one hamburger!"

"With cheese?")

"What are you doing?" I called at the top of my voice.

"I have a big test next period. I need to highlight my notes."

"Ah." I nodded, as if that explained it all. Next to Ashley two other girls in our grade that I'd seen around but never spoken to were studying their vocabulary books, trying to memorize 30 definitions before the next period. They were attempting to make up lame ways to remember each word and its respective definition.

"Vacillate," one girl read. "It's a verb. It means 'to swing indecisively from one idea to another, or to waver weakly in will or mind.' Okay, how can we remember that?" They sat in silence for a long moment, when suddenly the other girl jumped in excitement.

"I've got it!" she exclaimed. "Okay, listen close. This is a good one. Vaseline sounds like vacillate. Now Vaseline is slippery, right? If you slip on Vaseline, you'll swing indecisively." I almost choked on my pizza.

Tuesday my school had off because of a teacher's meeting. Emily's did as well. We spent our days at the barn, and both rode in the arena. It was kind of gloomy out, raining off and on all day. "Why couldn't we have a nice day off?" I questioned Emily as I put my left foot in the stirrup and climbed aboard Sultan. It was quiet all that morning, and you could just barely hear the rain pattering on the arena roof. All the horses were relaxed, even sluggish. Both Sultan and Angel were walking and trotting quietly around the arena when Sally entered leading Dawn. We all rode in contented silence, except for the occasional cry of "Rail!" to let someone know you were passing on the outside. Even Dawn, who was usually excitable, was relaxed.

"One of you pass me a couple times so she gets used to it," Sally requested. We all knew Dawn's phobia of horses passing her. Her ears would go back and either break, stop, buck, or go sideways. "Watch yourself," Sally called as Sultan and I came up next to her, a safe distance away from Dawn's flying hooves. When I was finished riding I patted Sultan on the neck. "Good job, girls." Sally dismounted. "You both had nice rides today."

"Dawn's getting better with other horses," I commented, sliding off as well.

"Yeah, she's getting there," Sally rubbed the mare's face, and then led her forward. Emily and I followed suit with Sultan and Angel. When I had Sultan cross-tied I went to glance out the barn door. It was raining again. I sighed. "Oh well." I was rolling up Sultan's leg wraps when I saw Sally at the end of the aisle glancing in at Major. I walked down halfway. "They said in another two months or so we can start hand walking him and turning him out in the small paddock." She glanced at me, but seemed to be fighting something. I nodded, stuck my hand through the bars to pet his nose. *He'll need to have his leg re-radiographed before that. Just to make sure everything's going all right...* I thought to myself, remembering the vet's orders.

"Must be hard for a horse to be cooped up in a stall so long," I commented.

"Especially a horse like him," she agreed. "In the end all

the medical treatment in the world can only do so much."
She walked away down the aisle. I knew what she meant
now. The sooner Major could walk around the better. Being
in a stall too long wasn't good for any horse. They got bored.
They got impatient. They got dull and listless. Horses
weren't made to be cooped up. How was he to know it was
for his own good? I patted him once more and started
toward the tack room where I'd dropped my large, hooded
sweatshirt. I'd known it would be too hot to ride in, but now
that I was off, and the rain was still coming down, I was
getting chilly. Emily was in there hanging up Angel's bridle.
"I called Anne," she turned toward me. "She's coming out to
drive Triumph when the rain lets up a little bit. She can drive
us both home."

"Okay," I nodded, remembering how lucky Emily's sister
was to be able to come and go from the barn as she pleased.
Being out of college and on her own she had freedom neither
of us could even imagine. But, I consoled myself, like all
adults, she also had work. At the moment she was working
part time, but her real job would begin in March. Emily and
I had grabbed two buckets, a few old *Saddle & Bridles*, and
some tack catalogs, and were sitting outside our horses' stalls
when Claire arrived. She ran up to us. "Hi!" she called,
breathless as always.

"Hey," I said, beginning to make room on my bucket for
her, but she immediately stepped into Sultan's stall. My big,
black horse lowered his head so she could pet him. I raised
my hands in defeat, pretending to be annoyed. Emily
laughed.

"Horses first," she said. I knew it was true. Sultan was all
over her, in her hair, bumping her with his nose. I shook my
head in wonder, closing my magazine.

"Are you riding Sly today?" I asked,

"Yeah," she scratched Sultan on the neck. "I'm riding
later."

"If he's cool you can turn him loose." I motioned to

Sultan, and watched as she unclipped the cross-ties and let them drop to the stall sides. She slid his door shut after un-haltering him and hanging it on his door. "How's Major?"

"Major's about ready to get outside, move around and be a horse again," I said to her. Claire nodded seriously.

"He's tired of standing around."

"Did he tell you that?" Emily smiled. Claire nodded again.

"Yes, he said if he has to stand around much longer he's going to stop caring." I glanced up sharply.

"Stop caring about what?" She shrugged and picked up my magazine. At that moment Sally came down the aisle.

"Do you girls want to take Major for his first walk today? It's a little earlier than the vets prescribed, but sometimes you have to go with your gut instinct." I stood up.

"Sure, but didn't the leg have to be re-radiographed before we walked him?" Sally nodded.

"The vet did that yesterday. I called." Shaking my head, I followed Sally and Claire to Major's stall. I never ceased being amazed by horses, or Sally. I just wished I could understand them as well as she did. Sally opened the door and handed me the halter and lead rope. Major turned and looked me straight in the eye. "Do you want to go for a walk?" I asked him. It didn't appear to me that I was getting any response. Sally and Claire said nothing. Getting Major out of the stall took some doing. Sally got behind him, I led him, and Claire stood in front, coaxing him along. Finally the four of us were standing in the aisle. I gave the liver chestnut gelding a strong pat on the neck. I saw that Anne had arrived and was tacking Triumph with Emily's help.

"I'll be right there, girls!" Sally called. To me, she said, "Just walk him up and down the aisle, maybe into the indoor, once Triumph is hooked and going. Only for about five minutes or so. Don't over do it." I nodded and clucked to Major. He followed Claire and I down the aisle, not willingly, but neither did he fight us. When Anne led little black Triumph out of her stall, though, Major halted. His ears came forward and he raised his head a little.

"That's Triumph," Claire explained to Major, giving him a kiss on his nose. We walked forward with him, heading toward the indoor arena. I halted Major at the doorway, and he stood, entranced, as Triumph trotted elegantly around the arena, Anne in the cart guiding her with the long reins. Major snorted once, then again. He reached out and bumped me with his nose. "Hey!" I protested, but really I didn't mind. When Triumph halted near him Major stepped forward. Sally took a hold of Triumph and let them touch noses. They both remained perfectly still until Major suddenly swung away.

"The rain stopped," Claire explained. "He wants to see outside." Sure enough, I listened, and no longer heard the steady drumming of rain on the roof.

"Well, take him to the door in the aisle." Sally instructed, leading Triumph off, back to the rail. I clucked to Major and we led him out of the indoor arena and turned right. Claire shoved open the big sliding door. Major raised his head sharply and snorted, taking a trembling step forward. The ground was soaked, but no rain was falling. The sun was just returning to the sky and the three of us stood in wonder for a few silent moments, Major most of all. I was the first one to move, remembering Sally's limit of five minutes. "Come on big guy, we've got to get you back to your stall. But don't worry, since you did so well, you'll get out every day now." Back in his stall he lowered his head and gave what seemed to me a big sigh. Yet, for some reason I couldn't help but feel that things were looking up. Anne was still driving when we finished with Major, so Claire and I hung out until they were done. When Anne led Triumph back to her stall to unbridle her, we all gathered by the doorway. Sally turned to Emily and I. "Well, I'm going to help Claire tack up Sly, so I'll say bye to you all now." We said our goodbyes and the two headed to Sly's stall. Anne ducked the cross-tie, and handed the driving gear to Emily and the bridle to me. We set out to return them to their proper places. Anne patted the pony's neck one last time and turned her loose in her stall.

"Alright girls. Ready to head out?" We followed her to the car and climbed in the back seat, since the passenger's seat was occupied by a jacket, purse and another bag.

"How about stopping for lunch?" Anne asked, glancing at the clock in the car as she pulled out of the driveway. Emily glanced at me and said, "Sure. Can Maria call her house and let Jessica know she already had lunch?" Anne passed her cell phone to the back seat and I dialed. Jess said that was fine, so the three of us began searching for somewhere to eat.

"Go left," Emily ordered.

"That's not the way to Maria's h…" Anne began to protest.

"Go left!"

"Alright," Anne gave in and swung the car left. We drove for a bit and it started raining again. We appeared to be on some back country road in the middle of nowhere. "I don't know why I let you talk me into these things. I don't even know where we are. I don't see any road signs and there's no restaurant around here…" Emily and I glanced at each other again and laughed. We drove around aimlessly for a bit. Anne made a few more turns and we could see civilization in the distance. We could also see a little diner on the left-hand side of the road.

"Turn," Emily demanded. I thought Anne was going to snap back at Emily for being bossy, but all she said was,

"Who's driving here?" But she turned, pulled into the empty parking lot, and we all climbed out of the car. "Millie's Diner," Anne said, reading the sign. "Nice choice, Em." She set off for the door.

"Well that was sarcasm if I ever heard it," Emily muttered, walking by my side. A plump, cheerful woman greeted us the second we entered through the swinging door.

"Right this way, dears." She led us to a table by a window and handed out menus. I noticed the place was totally empty except for us.

Chapter 8

"I think that was Millie," Anne whispered under her breath, and Emily kicked her under the table. She was enjoying our little outing. After bringing our drinks, 'Millie' (at least that's what we called her) walked away, and having nothing else to do but wait on us, she sat down on a stool by the bar. It didn't take long to decide what we wanted; our choices were pretty limited by the small menu. The second we set our menus down Millie was right back at our table, paper and pen in hand. It was sort of unnerving. She took our orders and left speedily. Emily drummed her fingers on the table to the music floating through the air. It didn't take long for our food to arrive, either. We thanked Millie as she set down our plates.

"So anyway, did Major enjoy his walk?" I heard Emily ask as I bit into my roast beef sandwich.

"Wow this is good...oh sorry," I apologized, laughingly, "Yeah, Major was very happy to get out of his stall," I nodded, "very happy. Sally said that soon she's going to start turning him out in the little paddock by the back shed." I took another bite of Millie's Special Roast Beef. "Jeez, Em, this was a good choice. Did you know it was here?" Emily just smiled and Anne shook her head. The place was still deserted when we finished Millie's Humungous Scrumptious Pies and got our humungous check that wasn't so scrumptious.

"On regular days this place is so crowded I don't get a moment to sit down, so today was a nice change," Millie told us, as she handed us our change. Emily walked the tip back to the table, although we might as well have just told Millie to keep the change since for all I knew she was cook, waiter and cashier. But she walked it back anyway, and we headed out the door. Looking back at the sign reading "Millie's Diner" I had to laugh.

✦

The days passed and turned into weeks. March came and went. Everyone at the barn was preparing for show season. Major was enjoying his turn out time, and now that he was no longer confined to his stall, he grew slowly but steadily better. The vets were amazed by how quickly his healing progressed. Sally was hesitant to begin turning him out, but once again she told me that healing the gelding's leg would be pointless if we lost his spirit along the way. He improved. All the kids took turns taking him on walks around the farm, feeding him peppermints, and generally fussing over him. Claire, though, I noticed, had taken a special interest in him.

It was the middle of April and I was just unbridling Sultan in his stall when I heard Sally talking to someone further down the aisle. I waited as Sultan dropped the bits from his mouth, and hung the show bridle on his door for a moment as I slipped on his halter. Then I stepped out of the stall and looked down the aisle to see Sally walking toward Major's corner of the barn with a woman around her age. The other woman was on crutches. I turned back to Sultan and gave him a kiss on his nose. "That must be Carol, buddy." I stepped to his left side to undo his girth. By the time he was totally un-tacked and I had put my stuff away, they were heading back up the aisle. I stood with Sultan, feeding him a peppermint, pretending not to be interested. "Oh, Carol, this is Maria. She's been helping a lot with Major. Maria, this is Major's owner, my friend Carol." I reached out to shake her hand, feeling dumb when she had to balance with the crutch under her arm as we shook. Sultan stepped forward as far as he could against the cross-ties. "And who are you?" Carol asked, as she again leaned her weight against one crutch and reached out to touch his nose. I felt better then.

"That's Sultan," Sally explained, "Maria's horse. He's registered as CH My Majesty." Carol said nothing; just let Sultan sniff her hand. I lowered my eyes again, not knowing what to say. Sally put a hand on Sultan's neck for a moment, and then suggested that Carol follow her back to her office.

"Nice meeting you, Maria. You too, Sultan," Carol called. Once again they headed down the aisle. I sighed and began currying Sultan's neck. I curried, brushed, combed, and was just reaching down to pick his left front forefoot when Sally returned, alone this time. I glanced up, "So?" Sally shrugged.

"Same thing as last time, she still blames herself, still wants to keep him here."

"I don't understand that....how she blames herself."

"I don't really, either, but I understand where she's coming from, I guess." Sally pushed Sultan's nose out of her hair. "Do you want to take Major out to the paddock when you're through here?" she asked. I nodded.

"Sure, just let me finish picking his feet." It didn't take me long to finish, as there was rarely anything in Sultan's hooves due to his pads and show shoes, but I checked anyway. When I was through and he was happily munching on his left-over hay from breakfast, I headed to Major's stall. To my amazement the gelding nickered softly and raised his head. "Hey, boy. I guess you're ready to get outdoors again." I slid on his halter, and he eagerly followed me down the aisle and out the door to the paddock gate.

When I unclipped the lead rope Major let out a loud snort, and took off at a trot across the hard ground. "Easy, buddy," I warned. He halted when he reached the other side of the tiny paddock, and stood stock-still for a long moment, then began eating what grass there was in the tiny enclosure. A little thrill ran through my body. Major was happy to be outside. And he'd trotted a little. Things were definitely looking up. But I had to wonder what would happen to Major once his leg healed. He'd probably never jump again, we knew that, or at least not competitively. What would Carol do? Would she ride him again? I turned from the gate my chin was resting on and headed back down the path to the barn pondering all this. I would have liked to stay with Major longer, just to sit out there with him, but I had to get a move on. It was spring break and I was heading to Emily's house to spend the night. I grabbed my bags from the locker room as my mind kept reeling. I said goodbye to Sultan. Emily was just pulling up in the van. I waved to Sally, reminded her that Major was still in the paddock, and climbed into the Dorman's blue van. "How was the dentist?" I asked, dropping my bag on the floor. She rolled her eyes.

"Fabulous, I just love having someone poke around in my mouth. But good news, as of now, no braces."

"All right," I said, happy for her. She hadn't wanted to get braces. The conversation continued all the way back to her house. When we arrived we unloaded my stuff and stood still for a moment.

"So what do you want to do?" Emily asked me.

"Anything," I shrugged, "I don't care." Emily set out toward the kitchen, and pulled out three baskets of strawberries and a large tray. She also brought out chocolate.

"We have a ton of strawberries my aunt brought over," she

explained. "We don't usually have this many strawberries sitting around. But do you want to make chocolate covered strawberries?"

"Are you kidding? I love strawberries!"

"I know, that's why I suggested it. I'm just good like that," she playfully whacked me on the head. As we washed, dipped, and set the strawberries on trays, we talked. I told her how much better I thought Major was doing.

"But what is he going to do when he does get better?" I let her in on the question I'd been pondering all day, as I sampled a strawberry, although the chocolate hadn't yet hardened.

"Yeah, does Carol even want to ride anymore? If she did would she do huntseat? I mean, just on the flat, obviously they wouldn't jump."

"I doubt it," I shook my head, "his head carriage isn't right, and he has too much motion for a hunter horse, really. He just happened to be an awesome jumper. I was thinking…Saddleseat."

"Really? You think Carol would do that? Ouch!" Emily poked herself with the knife, trying to take the green part off of the strawberry she was sampling.

"She used to," I shrugged. "But I, uh, wasn't thinking of her riding him."

"What, you want to ride him?" Emily laughed.

"Well, yeah, but no. That's not what I meant. I was thinking of a little blonde girl we know without a horse. But don't say anything yet."

"Of course I won't," Emily smiled. "But I think Claire riding him is a great idea!"

"Do you? Good." I was relieved. "He's such a sweetie, you know. And she's a good little rider for her age."

"Yeah, she really is. She does such a good job with Sly, who is totally uncooperative, with an attitude to boot. I don't know that she'll ever be able to show him. I heard Sally talking about that the other day. Sly gets so strong at a show.

All he'll want to do is rack, rack rack. And she's good, but she's just so small physically. You know?" Emily pulled out the last strawberry from the washed pile.

"Yeah, I know." I opened the next pack and began washing. As I did, the latest *Saddle & Bridle* caught my eye. It was on the bottom of the pile of mail further down on the counter, peeking out from under some junk mail. "Hey, can I see that?" I asked. "We didn't get ours yet."

"What? Oh yeah, sure." Emily kept dipping as I wiped my hands off and ripped open the large paper envelope, pulling out the thick horse magazine. A brilliant bay face greeted me on the cover. "It's good to see him back on there," I commented, holding the magazine up for Emily to see across the kitchen.

"Man, I miss that boy, but at least he's home now," Emily smiled. I nodded.

"What an adventure that was."

"Night Watch. What a horse that was." Emily put the final strawberry on the wax paper on the long pan and kicked the refrigerator door open with her right foot. She slid it onto one of the racks and turned around. "Do you realize our first show is only a few weeks away?" she suddenly demanded.

"Yeah, I know. The question is will Angel even recognize you after you've missed so many lessons?" I joked.

"Of course she will. And I plan to make that up this week anyway, since we are off school. You and I will be at the barn every day!"

"Does Sally know that?" I grinned.

"Yes, she does." Emily confirmed with a sniff.

"Well that's news to me, but good news!" I grinned.

Chapter 9

Those days in April were perhaps some of the greatest days I spent at Sunny Ridge Stables. They were gorgeous; it was early spring, and everything was coming alive again. The trees were growing buds, the grass was turning green, birds sang in every tree, and a light breeze ran through everyone's hair. It was warm and sunny and all of my friends gathered every day at our favorite place on earth—the stable. We helped with chores in the morning and relaxed by the big maple tree next to Major's paddock during lunch, instead of eating in the lunchroom above the barn. We rode in the afternoons. We would spread a large horse cooler on the ground beneath the tree and turn Major out in the paddock, as we shared stories and traded our lunches. We found that Major loved Fritos but wouldn't give raisins a second thought. Oddly enough though, he found grapes to be tolerable.

One day Tina brought a watermelon, and we held a seed-spitting contest. Major enjoyed the rind until Claire announced that the other horses were jealous and Major was willing to share. We found Sally and got her permission to distribute the leftover rinds to the horses throughout the barn. When we headed back to the paddock we found Snickers, the dog, enjoying the remainder of our lunch. Claire got sprayed with the hose for that one. That was the hardest laugh I'd had in a long time.

Then there was the day that Emily and Tina wanted to hold a race between the golf cart and the riding mower. We drew straws (real pieces of straw!) for who got which vehicle. Emily and I ended up with the lawn mover, and Tina and Sam got the golf cart. Eric stood as the starter, and dropped his hand as the starting signal. Claire sat on the paddock fence with Major, and I could swear both of them were laughing. No one was laughing when the race was over and the winners accidentally backed the golf cart into a tree, but smiles returned when we realized there wasn't a scratch on it.

On the second to last day of spring vacation, everyone showed up. Tina, Sam, Eric, Emily, Christine, Amanda, Tara, Claire, and I rode in groups. Later while the younger two played hide-and-seek tag, we sat around in a circle playing card games, including a game Sally's mother had taught us called "Donkey" which involved clothes pins, cards, and lots of screaming. Tina and Eric ended up having a small wrestling match over the last clothes pin.

The final day for me arrived, and Emily, Tina, Eric, and I were the only ones around. We begged Sally to let us take the lesson horses out bareback and ended up making a deal: we'd clean the tack room, and then take the ride. We worked quickly but efficiently, and the room looked great by the time we rushed to claim our mounts. I raced for Gypsy's stall, grabbed two lead ropes and snapped them to either side of her halter, before leading her out of her stall. Emily and Tina were attempting to ride Merlin double, and Eric was mounting Bambi. I counted to three, and jumped as high as I could, but realized Gypsy was still too tall to mount without stirrups. I knew how to vault onto a horse's back but didn't think Gypsy would appreciate it very much. She was around 16 hands, and although she was a 15-year-old lesson horse, she was still shown in Show Pleasure at some major shows. Vaulting onto her back would surely result in getting myself unceremoniously bucked right back off. I held her with my left hand as I dragged the mounting block over. She snorted, but stayed parked out while I arranged it and stepped on. From there I could hoist myself up onto her broad back.

Eric was just asking Bambi to walk off as well. She was the youngest lesson horse; a good natured mare who would do almost anything. She was bouncy and full of life, but very trustworthy with the younger set. Emily and Tina had made a good choice riding Merlin double. He was 20 years old, and every Sunny Ridge rider had begun on him. He was what some call "bomb-proof." He no longer showed, but still had a full lesson schedule. He was in great shape for his age, and at the moment was getting a little impatient with all Tina and Emily's bumbling around.

When we were finally all settled on our horses, I yelled, "Gypsy's leading!" and clucked to the mare who jogged eagerly across the grass to the pasture. Luckily the gate was open and the pasture was dry, so chances of pulling a shoe were slim. I glanced back to check on the rest of the party, and let Gypsy move into a real trot. Her ears were forward and she moved smoothly. Bambi moved up on her left and Merlin on her right, and for awhile we trotted three-abreast.

Suddenly Emily nudged Merlin with her heels, Tina clucked, and Merlin lurched into a canter. "Easy," I said to Gypsy, "Easy, girl." At that moment I wished I had a bridle on her. Bambi's trot had quickened as well, to the point that neither Eric nor I could post anymore. I looked at him; we both shrugged, grabbed some mane, and turned them loose. We were cantering across the pasture after Merlin when Sally stepped out of the barn. I would've stopped Gypsy but I doubted I could anyway, and Sally was actually smiling.

"Just don't fall off!" she yelled. I raised one hand in a half-wave, and then quickly dived down for more mane. Gypsy did stop when we reached the other side, gave a loud snort, and began doing something equivalent to a park walk in the showring. I rested my hands on her withers and asked her to "please chill out." She danced some more. Merlin had come right down from his lumbering canter to a halt where he was cropping grass. Bambi was even flat walking. "And I picked you, you nutcase." But I had to laugh, especially when I realized that Sally was video-taping. We played a round of Follow the Leader, Simon Says, and then took off at a trotting race across the pasture. We were almost through when Sally called that she wanted to see who could get their mount to canter a serpentine. Emily and Tina tried first, and it would've been fine since Merlin knew every pattern in the book. But he was more interested in eating grass than cantering, and he kept falling back to a trot and diving his head down. Bambi wasn't so great at patterns yet, but Eric did a decent job of getting her through it. I moved Gypsy forward feeling confident. I'd ridden this mare countless times before I'd gotten Angel. I'd practically taught her patterns. Granted, I'd never done one in the middle of a pasture bareback before with only a halter and lead rope, but....I shifted my weight, touched with my leg, and said, "Canter!" Four perfect halts and four perfect transitions equaled four perfect half circles.

"Nice one!" Tina called. She was the barn's resident equitation rider. I could tell that Sally agreed.

"Way to go, girl," I patted the mare's neck. We set out across the pasture one final time at a walk, heading back to the gate. Gypsy was relaxed now, and she actually lowered her head and flat-walked. When we reached the barn I slowly slid to the ground and stretched my muscles. "Well, that was fun."

"Are you kids happy now?" Sally asked, approaching the three horses. "Ready to go back to school?"

"No!" I said quickly.

"Well, I'm not ready for you to go back, either. I'll miss

having you kids around. Who else can back my golf cart into a tree and put it back without a scratch on it?" I stopped in my tracks and caught Tina's eye, but laughed when I saw Sally smiling. "Come on, let's get these guys back into the barn."

Chapter 10

The days, as much fun as they had been, ended, and brought the end of spring break. I found myself once more walking through my school's front door. I was not eager to be back, but the choice was not mine. For a moment my locker combination escaped me, but it came back as I began turning the dial. I exchanged the books in my bag for what I'd need for my first two periods and stood gazing at the snapshot of the "barn crew" and the computerized copy of myself on Sultan hanging on my locker door. The halls were beginning to get crowded now. I slammed my locker door shut and headed to homeroom. As I listened to morning announcements I realized with a jolt that our first show was only a week or so away. Usually before Easter, the show had been changed to after Easter this year for reasons beyond my understanding. Although the date had been made later, it was still a shock to be coming upon the show season so soon! In my mind I counted the horses and ponies that I figured would be showing there. I went over the barns that regularly attended, and decided that Sultan and I had a good chance at the Jr. Exhibitor Three-Gaited class. By the time I was seated in first period, I had decided that I'd better stop thinking about it or I'd never make it to any of my classes on time. I had walked to the wrong room and had to walk swiftly and dodge people to make it to the right one before the bell rang once more. But hey, it was the first day back. Algebra. I hated it. X, Y, and Z were my greatest enemies. Solving equations wasn't too bad if they were by themselves, but writing equations from word problems...that was torture—and that was what we were learning. The problems were all about Sue, Paul, Brad, and their little world. Their little problems were so amazingly complicated that I ventured to guess that nothing like that would ever happen to me in my lifetime. If I wanted to split up a jumbo chocolate chip cookie between three friends, I would estimate how much a third was. You're friends after all; you won't go strangling the person who got two centimeters more cookie. I worked on the next problem, wondering why I should be unfairly solving their petty problems. "Why doesn't Sue get together with Paul and Brad and the three of them figure out the answer?" I muttered, scribbling away. I totally confused myself when I ended up with my second answer as 32 ½ people fit onto each bus. "I guess it's better than a quarter of a person," I shrugged. I was relieved when the period bell rang and I could pack away my Algebra books. I shoved them into my backpack and zipped it closed. As I stood up and headed out the door I heard Mr. Morris call, "Finish up those problems for homework everybody!"

"Great," I muttered, threading my way through the crowd to get to English class. "This looks like one of those days where you get homework in every subject." First days back usually were. I survived English, World Studies, and all my other classes and true to my word, got homework in every one of them. I rode the bus home and began my work right away. I couldn't risk my grades dropping now, not with show season just beginning. I opened my hated Algebra book and began. "Sue, Paul and Brad want to build..."

"Finally." I stepped out of the car and onto the soft grass

at the Quentin Riding Club, surveying the old shows grounds that I knew so well. I zipped my jacket up to my chin as a cool breeze whipped by. The day was overcast and cool now, but it was supposed to warm up as noon came around. My dad unlocked the trunk, and Jess and I gathered our riding gear. I held my suit, hat, make-up box, and boots and headed for our regular stabling area. Tina was the first to greet me.

"Jeez, it's cold," she said as I dumped my things in a pile and hung up my suit.

"I'll second that. I could go for some…"

"Hot chocolate?" Emily poked her head into the dressing room and shoved a metal thermos into my hands.

"Thanks, Em." I took a grateful sip.

"Yeah, so we've all decided that no one should get changed into their suits until right before their class, or they'll freeze before they're even on the horse." Emily babbled as we stepped back into the aisle.

"Where's Sultan?" I asked as we headed between the rows of horses.

"Third on the right," Tina answered helpfully. My big gelding gave me a low nicker as I opened his stall door and stepped inside. I saw Sally heading up the aisle in what appeared to be about 20 huge layers of clothing.

"She should live in the south," I joked.

"Horse shows ought to be illegal when it's this cold out," she said to us as she passed. I laughed and backed out of Sultan's stall.

"It's supposed to warm up," I called after her helpfully. All I got was a shrill laugh in return. "I take it she doesn't believe me."

"No, she doesn't believe the weatherman." Emily replied, sipping more hot chocolate. "Do you really?" I glanced at Sultan again and watched him blow out of his nostrils. I could see his breath.

"No, I guess not." There were a bunch of in-hand classes

that morning, then the lead-liners. Since none of our horses were showing in-hand, and none of our junior exhibitors were young enough for a lead line class, we had no one showing until about quarter of 10 when Eric showed Irish in Show Pleasure Junior Exhibitor. Not long after that, Holly Fox, an adult exhibitor from whom I'd purchased Sultan, took her young gelding Milo in the Show Pleasure Driving class. It was getting on toward eleven o clock, when Claire arrived. She asked who had shown already, how had they done? Who was going next? I answered her questions as I led Irish up and down the aisle with a cooler draped over his back to cool him out safely and gradually in the frigid weather. I glanced at the younger girl wearing only a sweatshirt. "Aren't you freezing?" I asked.

"It's not that cold outside anymore," she replied.

"Isn't it windy?" I pushed Irish's nose out of my hair.

"Yeah," she explained patiently, "but the sun's warm." I pulled the cooler back a little and placed my hand on the horse's chest to see if he was cool enough to return to his stall. He was. Holly and Milo had just returned, and Emily was heading the horse as Sally and Rachel, her assistant trainer, unhooked the cart. I watched from the doorway.

"Maria," Dad called, crossing the aisle, "why don't you go and get something to eat? It's almost lunchtime." He held out 10 dollars.

"Umm…" I pulled him aside so that he wasn't in the way of the prancing youngster and watched as Emily led Milo into the barn.

"Walk. *Walk*." She repeated as the young horse danced along and then dropped his head in a half-hearted attempt to nip her fingers.

"Em, if I go for lunch do you want anything?"

"Umm, no I have some…" Her voice was cut off as she turned with Milo into his stall. I took the money.

"Sally, do you need anything right now?" I asked.

"Nope, we're under control." She was standing with Holly

demonstrating some point about how Milo needed to be driven, moving her hands wildly as she spoke.

"I ate on the way here, but I'll come with you," Claire said.

"All right." I stepped into the sunlight. It really had warmed up a little. But there was still a breeze, and I still wouldn't want to walk around in only a sweatshirt like Claire was, but the sun was definitely out. We strolled leisurely across the green grass and passed the parked cars. I was lost in a reverie when I was suddenly jolted back to the present by a voice beside me.

"Do you think…" Claire paused. "Do you believe Major came here for a reason?" I glanced down at her and smiled.

"Of course he did. Sooner or later we'll probably know why. And maybe we won't, but somehow between now and the…" I stopped and then continued, though it was hard to say, "the time he leaves, he will have fulfilled that reason."

"Well, I believe that," she declared as we neared the Chinese food stand. I always loved standing in line there. It was a good meeting spot for hungry exhibitors. I ordered some sort of rice thing with chicken and a limeade and we headed back. We stopped to let a few horses and riders heading down for a Walk Trot class parade by. As I stood there holding my food I studied the young riders and the trainers, watching as one halted the horse and helped his rider adjust her snaffle rein and switch her crop. I saw Claire's eyes wistfully follow the girl and her large liver chestnut Saddlebred as she clucked and they headed away. I put my arm around her shoulder and began to walk.

"Come on, kid." She followed along. She wasn't showing here. It had been agreed that Sly would not be suitable for a Walk Trot class, no matter how good of a rider Claire was for her age. He would just get too strong for her at a show, and she would be more likely to canter and rack her way around the ring than walk and trot. Her parents were searching for a horse within their budget that she could do well on, but hadn't yet found one. It was sad, too, because the only thing the girl wanted to do was ride.

I made up my mind right in that moment to tell Sally my idea. It couldn't do any harm. We rounded the corner of the barn to find a slight form of chaos. Whatever had been under control when we left was no longer. The relaxed, sleepy atmosphere I'd left was now uptight and on edge. Milo was being hand-walked in the sunshine by a thoroughly annoyed looking Emily. I made my way up to her and she shook her head. "Everything's out to get him today. Ooh, watch out Milo, it's an evil rock!" I detected a great deal of sarcasm in her voice. About to respond, I swung around upon hearing a loud "Heads up!" from inside the barn. Sally exited leading Wind Song, and I watched as she parted a large crowd of parents, adult riders, and younger siblings. She didn't even wait for a mounting block, leg up, or someone to head the horse; she swung aboard and let the gelding walk off, gathering her reins as she went. She did glance back over her shoulder once to make sure Tina was following close behind. I knew from past experiences that Sally usually warmed Wind Song up a bit before Tina got on to ride her class, but her class wasn't supposed to be for a while yet.

"What's going on?" I questioned, as Emily yanked Milo's head up from the grass.

"He's turning into a royal brat as he grows up, that's what's going on."

"No, why is Tina going already?"

"Oh! I forgot to tell you, they canceled a bunch of classes at the last minute. She's only got two classes before she goes and one has only one entry."

"Nice," I commented.

"Yeah, you might want to go check the schedule again and see how everything's changed. It messed everything up. As soon as I can get him back inside," she pointed to the gelding at the other end of the leather lead rope, "I'm starting to change into my suit." The group of onlookers had sort of dissipated now, most of them heading to the warm up ring or grandstands to watch Tina's class, yet the barn was still in a state of confusion. I could feel the tension bouncing off the walls as I skimmed the schedule stapled to the wall. I saw that due to all of the sudden cancellations, I didn't have long to get ready either.

"Shoot." I gobbled down half of my Chinese food, dumped the rest in the nearest trash can, and made my way to the dressing room. It was still slightly chilly in the barns, so I got my suit on as quickly as I could. I wiggled into my vest, and pulled my jacket back over it. "Brr." I shivered, stepping back into the aisle. Emily and I were both changed and ready by the time Wind Song returned. I was fumbling with two safety pins and my number, attempting to pin it straight on the back of my show coat, as Sally led Wind Song back to his stall. After poking myself with the pins a few times the number was straight, and I left it hanging up as I turned to Tina. "So how was your class?"

"Great!" she held up a red ribbon, second place.

"Awesome!" I gave her a hug. The normal feeling of anticipation was growing inside me now as I set about putting on my makeup and getting my hair in a neat bun. I found a crop, gathered my hat and gloves, and stood with Emily as we watched Angel and Sultan being led out of the barn together, tacked and ready to go.

"You two are so close on the schedule that you're just going to warm up together," Sally has said. So we got leg ups into the saddles and headed down the familiar path to the warm up ring. The ring was crowded, with horses going every direction, on the rail, off the rail, some halted in the center. In the middle of this typical melee, both Emily and I managed passes down the rail at a trot to warm up our mounts. In a minute Sally headed with Emily and Angel into the ring, and left Sultan and I standing with Rachel.

Sultan felt unfocused during our warm-up passes. Now he stood parked out chewing the bits and throwing his head around impatiently. The moments dragged and each passing second could've been a lifetime in my eyes; a lifetime of scratching Sultan's withers, taking deep slow breaths and straining my eyes to catch a glimpse of Angel's silvery grey form floating around the Quentin ring. A sudden wave of nervousness swept through my already tense body. Was I ready for this? Sultan sidestepped, growing impatient with all of the waiting, so I let him walk a circle. In another 10 lifetimes—or so it seemed—Sally was heading our way. Then it became a blur of shortening my reins, her taking his bridle and leading him out the gate and toward the show ring, tightening his girth, letting his long black tail down, and heading toward the in-gate at a strong trot. I relaxed the moment he took the first trot step, and he hit the ring feeling great.

Unfortunately that was the only time he felt great the whole class. He got stronger on the grandstand rail, fought my hold on the bridle, danced sideways like some kind of dressage move during the walk, and leapt into the canter the first direction. The second way of the ring was not much improved. I exited the ring exhausted, arms hurting from holding him back so much, and slightly annoyed with myself for getting nervous beforehand. I transferred all four reins to my right hand to accept the yellow ribbon with my left. Sally took it from me and walked along at Sultan's head as we moved slowly back to the barn. "Do you have any explanation as to why he did that?" she asked, and I detected half of a smile behind her neutral expression. I shook my head and looked away.

"It was me." She nodded.

"Partially, yes. But it was a combination of things," she waited, but when I was silent she went on. "To start with, it was his first class at the first show this season and you know he always messes up that class. Secondly, you were nervous. You don't usually get like that for me anymore, but occasionally you do, and it screws your horse up every time.

You've got to get over that. Lastly, the bit. He's never been shown in this bit before, remember?" I paused and remembered. It was true; we'd changed curb bits a month back. It had worked fine at home, in fact it had worked great, but apparently showing in it was going to take some getting used to. It was going to be a real challenge. I sighed.

"Yeah, I remember." Now she smiled for real.

"You have much to learn from him yet," she said as we halted in front of our barn. I waited, as she appeared to be on the verge of saying something else, but all she said was, "Okay, hop off."

The awards ceremony was just finishing up, and Carol slowed Major down from yet another victory canter. She threw her arms around his neck, as they exited the ring at a walk. People were congratulating them, patting Carol's knee, Major's neck, calling from across the aisle…everybody loved the big gelding, and even those he beat loved to see him win. Rumors were starting to fly about the Olympic Trials, and that Major and Carol were aiming at them. The Super Horse would have a new challenge.

Chapter 11

Time was what we all needed. I needed more time to work with Sultan before our next show, Major needed more time to heal before the show season was over so Sally could get Claire on him for at least one show that year. Sally needed time to get our plan underway without Claire knowing it quite yet. I had spoken with her at that first show as I promised myself I would, and Sally had patted my arm reassuringly.

"Trust me, my dear, that's part of the plan that's been forming in my head for a bit now." But then she threw in the curve. Carol now wanted to retire Major from showing of any kind and let him live out his days quietly in a pasture at Fieldstone Farm, the retirement farm outside of St. Louis. "I tried to explain to her that Major is not ready to retire and does not want to retire…" Sally sighed. "We'll see how it goes." There were other problems, too. The vets had worries. The weight of the show shoes, they protested, might put too much stress on the leg. It amazed me though, that we were even discussing riding and show shoes in the same sentence as Major, the horse that almost didn't live through the fall. But in a month he would be rideable and he was a

Saddlebred, after all…I couldn't yet believe his recovery. He was so ready to get back to really living again, and probably eager to jump again. Jumping was not an option we knew…but Saddleseat could be. If all went well, and we played our cards right, Claire would be on his back before the season was out. But we needed time, and time did not seem on our side. The moments moved on, drawing us further and further into show season. School let out for the summer, and gave me the time I needed to work with Sultan. But Major's time was measured differently, and I could only hold my breath and hope that everything would just fall into place.

With school out, I spent every day I could at the barn. I rode Sultan and took Major for long walks around the farm with Claire tagging along. My heart soared every time the gelding would become excited by something, flag his tail, and prance around me in circles. "After being inside for so long this must be Heaven," I commented to Claire during one such exhibition.

"He just wants to run again," she replied. "He's tired of walking, he wants to trot and canter like he used to!"

"Well, Major," I addressed the big horse, "you need to have patience. One more month. Just one month, and you'll be free to trot and canter."

To our amazement and delight, Major's healing had continued at a steady pace. And time did work with us, not against us. It was a few days into July, when Claire wasn't around, that Sally made the call. "Saddle Major," she addressed me. "Your saddle." I only paused a moment at this announcement, the one we'd been waiting for since the day he came to us back in the fall. I collected the tack I'd need and strolled to his stall, trying to keep my excitement in check. I set the saddle down in front of the door, hung up the bridle just like normal. I opened the stall door like I'd done countless times before. Yet the trembling excitement in my body betrayed me, and Major nickered as he raised his head from his hay.

"Yeah, boy, something is up. Here, let's get you cross-tied." I reached carefully for the ties and clipped them to both sides of his halter. As I set about brushing him, I felt my heartbeat quicken. This was the test ride, the sum of all our efforts throughout the past year. It was at this point that we sank or swam with our plan…and I would be the one riding him. I set down the brush and reached for the saddle pad. He stood absolutely still as I placed it on his back, followed by the saddle. I was girthing him up when Sally arrived in his doorway.

"Ready for this, old boy?" she gave him an affectionate pat. He took the bit eagerly when I began to bridle him, and followed me out of the stall, down the aisle, and toward the outdoor ring. I held the reins as Sally tightened the girth once more.

"Does Carol know he's being ridden again?" I asked. Sally glanced my way as she let the flap of the saddle back down.

"Carol knows it's about time for him to be ridden again, but she doesn't appear to be wanting to ride him. I'm going to see her again tonight and, depending on how this goes, I'm going to try and talk her out of this retirement idea. Depending on how *that* goes, I'm going to discuss a possible lease arrangement for Claire. All right, let's get you up there." She gave me a leg up, and as I gathered my reins I asked, "Why aren't you riding him, anyway?"

"I want to watch him move. All right, ask for a walk." I clucked and nudged my heels against his sides, and the big horse beneath me came suddenly alive. Working with him on the ground was one thing, but being on his back was just incredible. It wasn't really his size; he was no bigger than Sultan if that tall. His energy was just amazing, especially that first day. Even at the walk he flowed around the ring in an even four-beat gait. If he was moving lame in any way, I couldn't sense a trace of it. Sally's eyes scrutinized him critically. "How does he feel?" she questioned.

"Perfect," I replied honestly, a smile on my face.

"Okay, try an easy trot." She bit her lip. An "easy trot" was easier said than done. Major was bursting with excitement and had energy to burn. He jumped into a strong trot immediately at my signal. I shortened my reins and attempted to draw him back with,

"Whoop, trot. Easy, boy, easy." Reluctantly he slowed down, but his trot was everything a good Saddleseat horse's should be, and more.

"Fun, isn't he?" Sally saw the smile on my face.

"Yeah, he is."

"I know," she said.

"You rode him already?"

"Before the accident," she replied, "A few times over at Carol's place. She's my best friend, remember?"

"Right." I was sorry to bring him down to a walk. When Sally nodded as a signal to canter, I shifted my weight, touched with my right leg and hand and commanded,

"Canter!" I was nearly left behind when he dashed off, and I shortened my reins and held on.

"Slower!" Sally called above his pounding hooves. "Much, much slower!" I worked him slower each trip around, but she wasn't yet satisfied. "Slower!" she insisted, and suddenly it clicked. I lightened up, sat deeper, and pitter-pattered my hands on the reins. Something changed in Major then; his whole body grew light and airy, and the canter slowed to a floating, almost delicate gait. "There!" Sally finally approved. "That's his trademark canter."

"Wow!" was all I could say in reply.

"This horse has the nicest canter in the world," she declared, and I couldn't dispute that statement at all. The second direction we cut short so as not to stress his leg on the first ride, but Major was moving absolutely sound on the way back to his stall.

"I'll say that was a success at least," Sally patted his neck as she went to unbridle him. "I'm going to talk to Carol tonight and see what we can work out for you and that little girl," she addressed the horse.

I spent a fitful night and a few restless days wondering about Sally's talk with Carol. I called Emily to voice my concerns. "Oh, I don't know, Sally's pretty persuasive," Emily consoled me.

"Yeah," I admitted, "She is."

"Why don't you call Sally if you're so worried about it?" Emily suggested. I glanced at the clock beside my bed. 9:45. I couldn't. Not just because it was late. I just couldn't. It would have to wait until my next lesson.

My next lesson finally did arrive, and I had only been in the barn a few minutes when Sally approached me. I gave her a questioning look, and she proceeded to relate to me her visit with Carol and part of their conversation. "After hours of talking, she finally relented on the retirement issue," Sally said. Carol wasn't yet physically fit to ride, but more than that she wasn't mentally fit to ride. She still blamed herself. Having never been through such an event, I just couldn't understand how someone could feel that way about an accident. ("That's why they call it an accident," I had said to Emily, "because it wasn't anyone's fault!") Sally said Carol would come around eventually; she'd already gotten her over putting him down and now retiring him. But in the meantime, Major needed a rider, and Claire needed a horse. Carol agreed on the condition that we get the vet's "okay" and a second opinion from another vet. Both watched Major work and agreed he looked perfectly sound. They did, however, address shoeing issues.

"No big, fancy show shoes," one said. That was fine; he would be shown Walk and Trot, and had ample motion on his own, it didn't really need to be enhanced by a fancy shoeing job. Everything appeared to be falling into place.

Sally and I alternated riding him during the following week. Each ride was increasingly longer than the previous one as we attempted to rebuild his muscle tone. As he gradually regained his previously healthy state, I was finally able to look at the pictures in the photo album upstairs and see the resemblance. One thing was sure: the broken-down, dejected horse that had arrived at Sunny Ridge almost a year ago was long gone, replaced by the gorgeous and healthy liver chestnut that now stood before me. We had been riding him late in the afternoons once Claire had already left, but soon the time would come to try out our new pair.

Chapter 12

It was about one o'clock on a sultry July day when I caught up with Claire in the barn aisle. Over the noise of the big fan blowing cool air throughout the barn I told her Sally wanted her to go and fetch her saddle. "Okay," she shrugged, and dutifully set out to get her saddle from the tack room. Emily caught up with me as I was cross-tying Major.

"What's going on?" she questioned.

"Shh," I cautioned, "Just watch." I stepped back into the aisle and waved to Claire who was now walking down the stairs from the tack room with her saddle. She headed our way.

"In here," I pointed to Major's stall. She moved into his doorway and paused. "Well," I asked, "Can you saddle him or should I?"

"What?" her head swiveled my way as her eyes lit up. "I get to ride him?" Emily grinned at my side, apparently enjoying the scene.

"Yeah, you get to ride him. Here's a saddle pad. Let's get him tacked up." With Emily and I helping, Major was tacked and ready to go in a matter of minutes—just in time, too, as Sally strolled down the aisle just at that moment.

"What a surprise, huh?" Sally joked with Claire, who stood patting Major's shoulder to no end. The girl just kept smiling silently, even as Sally bridled the big horse.

"And she hasn't even heard the best part yet!" I whispered to Emily. Sally handed the reins to Claire and the whole group of us headed toward the outdoor. I closed the gate behind the horse and headed him as Sally legged Claire up into the saddle. Once the girl had gathered her reins, she turned to Sally awaiting instructions of some sort.

"Go ride," Sally said simply. So ride she did. Major floated around the ring for her in a way I doubted he'd even done for me. They were that sort of perfect pair...the kind you just know are meant to be, the kind that work together so perfectly and move together so beautifully. I saw that from the moment Major picked up the trot. Claire's smile only grew the more turns they took around us. When she halted Major in the center of the ring they were both breathless. Major was breathing heavily as he wasn't yet in great shape, and Claire was just bursting with excitement. She leaned forward and threw her arms around the gelding's neck, thanking him for the ride.

"Well, you could be thanking him for many more rides, if you'd like to," Sally told the already thrilled girl, who sat back up with interest. "How would you like to lease Major to show the rest of the season?" Sally asked with a smile.

"I'd love it!" Claire exclaimed, giving Major yet another hug. Emily and I looked on happily. At least all the work, all the planning, and all the dreaming hadn't been in vain. Major wouldn't jump again, but he seemed rather happy carrying Claire around the ring. Time would tell if girl and horse would make a great team, but if that first ride was any indication of what they were capable of, that was exactly what they were headed for. Claire reluctantly swung her right leg over the saddle and dismounted. Still smiling and talking, she and Sally headed toward the gate. Emily started after them, but stopped after two steps and turned back to me where I stood watching the trio walk away.

"What?" Emily studied my face.

"Darn, I'm good." I said with a laugh, shook my head, and walked forward after Emily.

✦

Carol was all dressed up in her riding attire, and Major was tacked up, ready to go. Jeff headed the horse, who stood calmly, watching with interest the commotion about him. "Are you gonna smoke 'em?" someone called to Carol from across the warm-up arena. Carol gave the rider a thumbs-up sign and urged Major into a trot. They warmed up the same way as always, in typical Major fashion, all rail work, and two jumps. He didn't need to practice.

As they waited for their turn, Carol's mind drifted back to the moment she'd decided to train Major as a jumper. "Two seasons," she'd told herself. "We'll just try it for two seasons." But the gelding was so talented, and he reveled in the excitement of jumping. To quit would've been a waste of his talent, and it wouldn't have been fair to him, either. So Carol and Major returned to the show ring each year, and Major continued winning. This day, though neither one yet knew it, would change the course for both of them, forever.

Their number was called, and Major trotted elegantly into the arena, as always, ears forward, showing off for his admirers. The crowd roared, and they moved into a canter, the buzzer sounded, and the pair started off on their last jumping course together.

Chapter 13

July flew by too quickly for my taste. It was the typical summer of riding, showing, and hanging out at the barn. It was soon the last week of July, and I found myself staring one of my last horse shows of the summer in the face. It was my last show before Louisville, and it was Claire's first time out with Major. Sultan and I had been improving steadily all season, and Claire and Major had been working hard at home preparing for this show. We were all looking forward to it when August 1st rolled around. I was humming to myself as I strolled happily down the barn aisle, headed for Major's stall. Claire was tacking him up for another practice ride in the full bridle. I paused in their doorway and leaned against the wall observing as she carefully wrapped his front legs. I laughed when he lowered his head as far as he could on the cross-ties and lipped up some of her wavy blonde hair. "Major!" she cried, standing up and moving across to the other leg. When she had saddled him and tightened the girth as much as she could, I picked up the bridle to help her get it on, since he was very tall and she was very short. It was a gorgeous show bridle with a maroon colored brow band, and he went with a simple, long shanked curb wrapped in latex, and a broken snaffle. I slipped it easily into his mouth, and buckled the throatlatch and cavesson shut. I tightened the curb chain to link two.

"There you are," I said brightly, handing the reins to Claire, who took them eagerly to lead him out to the ring. But something wasn't right. As soon as she stepped forward, Major, like any well-trained horse, would step forward to follow her. He hesitated for a moment, and then took a lurching step after her. I groaned. "Whoa, Claire, stop right there." Had I really seen that? Or was I just making it up because that was my worst fear? No, I couldn't be making that up; it was such an obvious lame step... "Don't move." I went to find Sally. I knew she wasn't in her office which was almost right across from Major's stall, so I raced up the aisle, not knowing why I was running because it wasn't as if it was going to get drastically worse in the few seconds it would take to get to her. I ran into her, literally.

"What's wrong?" she asked, upon seeing my face.

"Major...I think he's lame. Claire was going to lead him out of the stall and he kind of wobbled when he took a step. I told her to stop right there and wait for you." Sally swore under her breath and started quickly toward the end of the aisle. When we arrived Claire and Major were standing in the exact same spot I'd left them in.

"Lead him out, Claire," Sally instructed. Major stepped over the stall divider and into the aisle, and indeed he favored that left leg. Sally knelt down and ripped off the leg wrap, and felt the leg for heat or other signs. She told me to take off the other leg wrap. I did. She felt that leg, too. Then she stood back up. "Un-tack him and leave him in his stall, I'll call the vet and get him here as soon as I can," she said to me. "Claire, go take your saddle and tack up Sly." We all went our separate ways, Sally to her office and the phone, Claire reluctantly to Sly's stall, and I turned Major around and led him back into the stall he had just come out of.

I felt depressed. Was all our work now going down the

drain? The vets had suggested about a year's healing time before competition, unless there were set-backs along the way where he went lame or tender in that leg. *We've been lucky up until this point, I guess,* I thought as I unbridled the big horse. But now we weren't. Claire would be so disappointed. And what about Carol? Well, I didn't quite understand the lady; I didn't know if she cared one way or the other. She might blame us, or Sally at least. She didn't know me well enough and definitely didn't know how much influence I was having on her horse's recovery *(or what had been recovery,* I thought bitterly) to blame me for it. But Sally, she could blame. Would she? She had wanted to retire him, and if we hadn't stepped in and convinced her otherwise, Major's leg would not have been re-injured... she didn't even need to blame me. No one did, I threw enough blame on myself. I had agreed with Sally all the way.

Now was the worst time for a set-back, right when we were looking their first show in the face. But to all of us Major's long term health was more important to us than one show, even if it had been Louisville. I was upset and angry, but I didn't know who to aim my anger at so I slammed the bridle on the hook on his door. I chucked the splint boots across the aisle and felt a little better, except that they thunked against Simba's stall and made him jump about five feet. "Sorry!" I called to the friendly little pony. I snatched a curry comb and brush from the nearby wash racks, which were two stalls down from Major, across from the entrance to the indoor arena.

I began to curry his coat feverishly. I curried and curried and curried, my mind reeling at an amazing pace. *How could Major be lame? Why had he gone lame? We'd followed the vet's orders...well, except for starting the hand walking a little early, but we had to...*I don't know how long I stood there, currying his dark coat in a circular motion, but it was a long time before I remembered to pick up the brush. *The vets were just here to see him! They said he was perfectly sound. Perfectly sound!*

Look at him now, he limps terribly. What in the world went wrong? I gave the horse a little pat and sank down on the sill to his stall, closed my eyes and tried to think. What use was it? Thinking would change nothing. Nothing! He was lame, probably wouldn't get better for a long time, not in time to show at least, and maybe he even managed to re-fracture the bone or make it worse? And if it was worse it would be our fault! What could be done then? What were the chances of a P3 fracture healing *twice?* Did it really look that bad, though? Maybe he just used it a little too much between being ridden and turned out, or maybe he bumped it getting up from a nap in his stall. Maybe it was just sore. I'd never broken a bone. When you broke a bone did it get sore? I didn't know. My eyes flew open when I felt someone looking at me. It was Sally. She leaned down and pulled me off the ground. "The vet will be here in about an hour and a half. He's with a horse that caught itself in a wire fence right now," she grimaced. I nodded.

"Okay." I hesitated, "What do you think is wrong with it?"

"I don't even want to take a guess." She shook her head. Then she gave me a slight smile. "Just remember that even doing what we did with him so far was incredible," she said, and headed down the aisle. What was that supposed to mean? That even if we lost the fight now we should be happy? Did she really think it would come to that? She must've meant something else...she *better* have meant something else. I groaned for what seemed like the millionth time that day.

I was there when the vet came. He had Sally lead Major around a bit, then returned him to the stall. I hung out in the aisle and tried to hear him talking. Sally had told me that I could be there, but I wasn't sure if I wanted to be or not.

"It was healing so well…I don't think he fractured it again. I think he just needs rest, less stress on it for a while. Go back to hand-walking him, minimize his turn out, and wait a bit. See where that takes you. Once he's moving sound again, start with lunging and gradually work up to riding. It's hard to predict how long it will take to get him sound…you're kind of starting all over again." *Starting all over again! It had taken us a year to get to this point! Poor Claire.* She had found the right horse and still she wouldn't get to show. *Poor Major.* He wanted to go just as much as we wanted him to. Sally had told me that in his earlier show career he would throw a fit if Carol took horses to a show and he was left behind. Sally thanked the vet. He told her to call if there were any changes for the worse, and he headed back toward the sliding door at the end of the barn and out to his truck. Sally walked away and returned a moment later with a tube of Bute paste in her hand. She gave him 2 cc's to help with the pain in his leg and gave him a pat on the neck. Then she took him off the cross-ties and let him loose in his stall.

"We'll just have to slow down his training that's all," she said to me. "Go slower, and see where that takes us. For now he gets a break. We'll start up again once he's moving normally." I nodded dumbly.

"Right." That was when Claire came racing down the aisle, apparently having been sent off while the vet was visiting.

"How is he?" she asked, running to his door and peering in, as if to make sure he was still there and still breathing.

"He's fine, he just needs more rest and to relax for a few weeks before we start riding again."

"Oh, okay." Claire dropped down from her toes and unlatched the door to give Major a kiss on his nose. "I'm glad you're going to be okay. I was scared for you a little there."

The horse bumped his nose against her shoulder. I loved watching the two of them interact. My heart melted watching them.

Chapter 14

He wasn't getting better. We had given him a few days of stall rest, and then tried to hand-walk him as we'd done the first time. It felt like I was re-living those months over again, and I didn't like it. Sally and I had watched his leg as I led him down the aisle, and he had been just as lame as that day Claire had him all tacked up ready to ride. We returned him to his stall. Sally went immediately to her office and didn't come out for some time. I sat on a bale of hay at the end of the aisle, alone and dejected. *I should be concentrating on me and Sultan right now, planning for Louisville,* I thought to myself, knowing this upcoming show was my last practice show before the World Championships at the end of August. But instead my thoughts were lost thinking about Major and Claire and articular fractures...Sally strode purposefully down the aisle way toward me now. I stood up and gave her a questioning look.

"I called the vet again," she said, "and he's coming back out today, right now. We're going to try injecting that joint with acid. It's the last option to get him sound for the show."

"Right." I felt obliged to answer, although I really had no clue what this acid was or what it was supposed to do. Sally went on to explain a bit more about how it helps ease the friction between the bones in the joint, and the vets thought it could be helpful in Major's case. But it was tricky and not done too often, so it was always saved as a last resort. But this was indeed, our last resort.

So they injected his joint and we started over. First stall-rest, then hand-walking, then lunging, and turn-out…to my amazement the injection seemed to have helped, and he progressed steadily in the weeks leading up to the show. Sally had me ride him the first time he was to go under saddle since our set-back. Claire was not around; she was on vacation with her family and wouldn't be back until two days before the show began. I mounted with some trepidation, and asked him to walk off. He did, and I began to relax when he moved off smoothly. We walked and trotted that first day, and Sally waited another two days before riding him again. Once more, she put me on him and watched him from the ground. We circled her at the walk and trot and then did one short canter. When I felt his smooth, rocking canter I had to wonder how anything in the world could be wrong with a horse that moved like that. It was perfect, absolutely perfect. "He could have been a dressage horse!" I exclaimed, with a small laugh.

"He could've been anything," Sally gave his neck a hearty pat, "but I think he's pretty good where he is right now." I dismounted and led him back to the barn to unsaddle and bathe. Although his short jaunt around the ring wasn't a true work-out, it was a sultry August day, and I thought a cool bath would be nice for him. I fed him a peppermint after I was done, and stood gazing at that leg…that stupid leg.

The days flew by, and his improvement continued. I was sure, though, that showing was out of the question. Claire wouldn't even be able to ride him before the show, even if they did go. But I did notice that Sally still hadn't scratched the two from their classes she'd entered them in before Major had gone lame on us. She was still clinging to something. So, I put my faith in her once more, and continued to help with Major's progress. Emily and I took him out to lunge one day as Sally had asked us. I stood in the center holding the long lunge rope, and Emily sat on the fence, watching with interest. "He's not off or anything," she called.

"I know," I said, "thank goodness. But he shouldn't be, either, he hasn't been ridden much at all, just every few days." I made a face. "I don't know if it's that or that acid stuff the vets injected that's keeping him sound." Emily nodded.

"Well, I'd like to think it's the acid stuff and that he's healed for good now," she said brightly.

"Yeah, I'd like to think that, too...whoa!" Major halted and stood patiently, awaiting my next signal. I walked to him, reversed him, stepped back into the center, and gave two clucks. "Trot!" I commanded. He picked up his easy, floating gait.

"At least he was happy this time," Emily commented. She seemed determined to find a bright side to the whole situation. "Last time he was out of work he was miserable."

"Yeah, he's happy all right," I watched the horse's eager movements. He was happy. *But he'd be happier if Claire could show him. What is your problem?* A voice in my head demanded. *You should be thrilled the horse is happy and comfortable and moving without pain, not pouting because he can't go to a dumb show. It's only a horse show, after all.*

"Yeah, I know," I muttered.

"What?" Emily questioned from the rail.

"Nothing. Whoa!" I called, and Major stopped dead once again. What a perfect horse. I walked to his head, and led him to the gate.

Chapter 15

This time Emily was at my house. We had until six to pack my show things, then her parents were coming to pick us up. I was staying over at her house that night and we were leaving for the show the next day. We were actually driving to the barn first, and would be helping to load the trailer with Sally and Rachel, and then follow the horses up to the show grounds. It didn't make much sense to my dad. "Why can't I just drive you to the barn tomorrow morning around 10?" he asked. I had sighed impatiently, trying to sound as if he was being dumb and there was some very obvious reason, when in reality the reason was simply because I wanted to spend the night with Emily.

"Daaad," I whined.

"Whatever, if you really want to go with Emily, then go. I was just trying to save her parents some driving. I mean, really, why didn't you just bring your things to the barn today? Then you could've just gone home with her from there." I didn't say anything because my only answer was a bad one; I just plain hadn't thought of that. Emily and I were great at last minute planning. Parents on the other hand, didn't seem to understand that. But in the end Dad gave in, so Emily was lying on my bed, choosing my tee-shirts while I was rummaging through my closet, searching in vain for my top hat.

"I can't find it!" I wailed. "Here's my derby…here's my other derby…"

"You have another derby?"

"Yeah, my one from Walk and Trot…" I said distractedly. "We never sold it…"

"Oh." Emily pulled out a bright pink shirt.

"Oh you are so not packing that," I said, glancing over my shoulder.

"Why not? I think it's adorable."

"Well I happen to think it's hideous. Put it back." She ignored me and stuffed it in my duffel bag. "Emily!" I abandoned my search for the top hat and dove at the shirt. I crammed my hand inside the bag but she slammed her whole body on top of the bag so I couldn't get it out. "Okay, you know what? Just put it in, but I won't wear it even if you do."

"You will if I only pack a certain number of shirts and that is one of them." She grinned.

"Or I could just take the task of packing away from you and make you find my top hat!"

"Fine, fine. Take the pink shirt. But I don't see what's so awful about it." She chucked it across the room at me, and it landed pink and ugly at my knees where I was once again kneeling at my closet door.

"It looks like…like something that Little Bo Peep would wear. All you'd need is one of those funky hats, a staff, and a few sheep." I made a face at the lace around the collar. My grandma had sent it to me a few years back. Suddenly my hand struck gold. "I found it!" I cried, pulling the black hat box out from under a couple winter jackets that had taken a tumble off their hangers, probably sometime when I'd slammed the closet door a little too roughly. Emily was still in convulsions over Little Bo Peep, so she said nothing about the hat. I stood up and strolled over to my duffel bag. I checked out what she'd packed, zipped it shut, and tossed it at the pile by my door. "Let's see, duffel bag, suit bag, hat box, makeup box, boot bag," I checked off everything I needed. "I think I have it all." I glanced over at Emily, then picked up the shirt and threw it at her where it landed on top of her head. "There, *you* can be Little Bo Peep since she amuses you so much. Are you ready? Let's go." We both grabbed my things, and tromped down the stairs together.

We waited in the kitchen, eating leftover pizza cold from the refrigerator and drinking a mixture of Sprite and grape juice until her parents came. My Dad was in the living room watching TV, and Jess was up in the shower. Emily and I had not spoken about Major all night. We talked about Sultan and Angel and Timmy and Triumph, and just about every other horse in the barn. But neither of us mentioned Major, and we still hadn't when the familiar blue van of the Dorman family finally pulled up out front of the house, and the horn honked. We dumped our glasses in the sink and set out with my stuff. "Bye, Dad!" I called. "Say bye to Jess for me!"

"Wait a minute," Dad called back, coming out and meeting us in the front hall. "See you up there," he said, giving me a hug. "Have fun." He turned to Emily and gave her a hug too. Then we departed out the front door, loaded my things and seated ourselves in the van. I was excited for the show now; now that I was no longer at home it was starting to seem real to me. The night was warm, and we drove with the windows open to feel the nice breeze. It took about 20 minutes until we pulled up at Emily's house. I left all my show clothes and accessories in the van, and took only what I needed for the night inside. Neither Emily nor I were ready for bed. We played a game on the computer, watched some TV, and talked in her room while playing our favorite CD in the background. Finally, we fell asleep.

We awoke the next morning to the sound of voices downstairs. Her parents were up, and it sounded as if they were in the kitchen and someone was cooking. I heard pans clanking around. I rolled over on the air mattress on the floor of her room. "Emily." Silence. "Emily." I hated the sound of my voice in the morning.

"Mhhhmmm," she groaned.

"Emily."

"What?" She didn't open her eyes.

"It's nine thirty."

"So?"

"So your parents are making breakfast, and we need to get ready so we can get to the barn."

"Oh, okay." She opened her eyes and sat up. We dressed and headed down for breakfast. Her mother was making pancakes. I hadn't had pancakes in a long time. I loaded mine up with butter and syrup and set about devouring them. I had eaten two already when I noticed the powdered sugar. I sprinkled a little of it on my third one to test it out.

"Not bad," I mumbled to myself, taking a sip of my orange juice. When every pancake was gone and the orange juice jug was empty, Mrs. Dorman began clearing the table. Emily and I helped her out, and then began getting her show stuff and my overnight things ready to go to the van.

"Everybody ready?" her dad called, grabbing his keys. We nodded, struggling out the door with armloads of stuff. "Alright, then. We're off!"

We arrived at the barn by 11. The barn's trailer was already parked by the big sliding door, and it looked as though loading it had already begun. Sally, Rachel, and Frank, the barn's only groom, seemed to have the procession of stuff from the barn to the trailer underway. Some things were left in from show to show, but others had to be taken in and out every time. "Girls, you can grab all of the bridles and saddles. They're already in their bags," Sally called. "They're at the bottom of the stairs." Emily and I raced the few steps inside the barn to the staircase and collected as many bridles as we could in our arms on the first trip. We doubled back a few more times until each piece of tack was loaded in the trailer. We then began to help with the other things that needed to end up at the show, such as the stepladder, and the box filled with extra bits. Once all the non-living items were loaded, it was time to load the four–legged ones. We just had to wait for the transport to arrive. Twenty minutes later the big silver horse trailer creeped slowly up the driveway. Once it had parked and the driver had pulled down the ramp, Sally stood just outside the barn door reading off the list of horses in the order she needed them on the trailer. Emily, Rachel, Frank and I raced back and forth, snatching horses out of their stalls and placing their lead ropes in Sally's hands to lead up the ramp onto the big rig. Most of them were show ring veterans and good about loading, as well as everything else. Even Timmy, as young as he was, stepped calmly onto the trailer.

"Sultan, Angel, Major!" Sally called loudly, the names of the next three horses to be loaded. My pulse quickened. Major? I grabbed Sultan from his stall, and he walked eagerly along at my side, black ears swiveling from side to side, eyeing the truck parked outside. He, like the rest of the horses, was wearing a light scrim sheet over his back to keep away the dirt. *They must've already been washed for the show,* I thought. Once he was safely in Sally's hands, I headed back down the aisle for Major, giving Angel a kiss on the nose as I passed Emily leading her out. I slid Major's halter on and clipped his lead onto the ring. He, too, had a sheet on. Sally must've had some hope left.

He stepped out of the stall and followed me to the other end of the barn, clearly wondering what this was all about. I handed him off to Sally, who led him onto the trailer like everybody else. He loaded perfectly, and backed into his compartment without fuss. He was the last one on the trailer. They slid the ramp up and closed the door.

The day was hot, and the warm air rippled through the open window of the Dorman's van. We were following close behind the transport hauling the horses to the show. It was around 4:00 pm, and we were nearing the show grounds. I gave Emily, who was dozing off, a little shove with my elbow, and she sat up straight. Together we watched the last few miles flash by and began to gather our needed possessions in our laps as the van turned into the familiar Quentin driveway. It amused me how many shows we attended there, but I really loved the place, and we were lucky to live as close to the show grounds as we did.

When Mr. Dorman parked the van on the green grass, we hopped out right away and made our way toward our regular barn where the horse transport was now parking. Sally was already there speaking to the driver as he pulled down the ramp and laid out the mat. Between him and Sally, they unloaded the horses by leading them down the ramp, and handing them off to Rachel, Emily and myself. Rachel helped direct us to the stalls Sally had assigned them to. The stalls were already bedded, and the buckets and cross-ties were set in each stall as well. Rachel had been there all day setting up and the tack trunks were the only things that weren't yet unloaded.

Sultan was third off the trailer, and I took his lead rope and led him down the aisle to where he would be spending the next few days. Emily, upon instructions from Rachel, had begun tossing flakes of hay into each stall. I waited for her to slip Sultan his hay and then closed his door. He immediately began tearing at his food as if he hadn't eaten in days. When the last door was closed behind the last hungry horse, we stood around useless for a moment, awaiting the signal to unload the trunks. When it came, the dolly was pulled over to the side of the trailer, and together the bunch of us set two of the large wooden tack trunks on at a time. We wrestled them to their proper spots in the aisle and returned for more. I was happy when we were done—they were heavy! Emily and I leaned against the barn wall as Sally and Rachel spoke with the driver, thanked him, and sent him off.

"Well, girls, most of the work is done for now. I just want to start sanding feet. Frank washed all the critters back at home, so other than a brushing, some Show Sheen and hoof black, they're mostly ready." Emily's parents had driven us up to the show grounds the night before the show actually started so that Emily could get a practice ride with Angel in that afternoon. I would be staying with them at a hotel nearby that night, and Jess and Dad would be arriving the next morning. "When Angel's done eating most of her hay come get me, and we'll go ride," Sally had said to Emily. For now there was nothing Emily and I had to do. Rachel picked the first horse from its stall and cross-tied him in the stall used for grooming. Sally started up the sander and began on the first foot. I hated that fine, dusty powder. It made me cough, so I moved away and headed to Sultan's stall. He pricked his ears and began to raise his head from his hay, but then changed his mind and took another mouthful. Just then I heard a shout from outside the barn and a car door slammed. Claire came racing down the aisle toward me, arms outstretched. She threw her arms around my waist in a hug when she reached me, and I picked her off the ground, twirling her in a circle.

"What's up kid?"

"I'm so excited!" she blubbered. "I can't wait to ride! Where's Major?" I set her down and pointed her toward the right stall. She promptly set off toward it. Smiling, I closed Sultan's door and set after her at a walk. Claire was already seated cross-legged in Major's doorway, talking to him as he munched contentedly on his hay. "And then they'll ask us to walk for a little, and then we have to reverse and trot again..." I listened as she went through their class step by step. Emily arrived at my side in a moment, and announced that Angel was nearly done eating. She got Sally, who halted the hoof sanding process to join in tacking the grey mare. Sally legged Emily up into the saddle as I headed Angel, but the mare started to walk off anyway as soon as Emily's seat touched the saddle. I let her walk, and Emily gathered all four reins as she moved out. After years of doing it, it gets quite easy and almost becomes second nature. Sally walked on Angel's left side by her head, and Claire and I followed along on her right. We stood on the rail of the big oval ring and watched as Emily clucked to Angel and she moved into a flashy show trot. The chains on her front feet clinked as she passed by us, but oddly enough that was the only sound in the still afternoon. No one else was working horses, and she was alone in the ring for the moment.

Watching Angel parade around the ring I was swept back a few years...I was sitting aboard. She was mine, and so much was different. Not that I wanted that back again. That would mean never meeting Emily, Night Watch, never owning Sultan...A loud "Heads up!" snapped me back to the present as a cantering chestnut entered the ring pulling a cart.

"I don't think he's supposed to be cantering," Claire whispered in my ear.

"Bring him back to you!" shouted the "heads up" guy. "Bump him! Good! Snap that whip and NOW trot!" Claire and I grinned at each other. Angel and Emily were now cantering the second direction, dodging the chestnut in the cart and letting him have the rail. Sally held up her hand as a signal to quit, and Claire and I met them at the in-gate. Emily had her reins on Angel's neck and Sally gave the mare an appreciative pat.

"That was great, Em. Maybe we don't even need a practice

ride for you two anymore. Maybe we can just save her for her class."

"Maybe," Emily agreed.

When we had reached the barn, Emily had dismounted and Angel had been taken care of, the Dormans and I got back into the van to head to our hotel for the night. We were lucky, and our room was only on the second floor...the pool was right at the bottom of the stairs through some swinging doors! Emily and I unpacked our things and changed into our bathing suits. We went for a swim, then after showering, we fell asleep to music videos playing on the TV.

The next morning we were up by six a.m. and in the van by quarter of seven. We had stopped at McDonald's for breakfast, so we all arrived at the show munching on hash browns and egg sandwiches. We had dropped our show attire off the night before, so all I carried was a small backpack and my breakfast. I greeted everyone on my way into the barn between bites of my sandwich, and after tossing the paper bag in the nearest trash can, I examined the show schedule more closely than I had the previous day. It was a two day show, and I showed in the evening both days. Claire rode in the morning and evening on Sunday.

Well, I had all day to watch my friends show, shop, or whatever else I felt like doing. Only the day flew by faster than I ever thought possible, and I soon found myself struggling into my formal pants, shirt, cummerbund, and bowtie. I left my jacket off for the moment, but put a jean jacket on instead in an attempt to keep my white shirt clean. I made sure my number was on the back of my jacket, my lapels were pinned, and that my gloves, top hat, and crop were all handy. By that time Sultan was cross-tied, cleaned, and saddled.

His nose was shiny from the baby oil we always rubbed on it. His bridle was hanging on the hook by his door. I glanced at the curb bit. Our past few shows had been a drastic improvement over our first one in that bit. Hopefully this would go well…My wishing was shattered by the announcer blaring the first call for my class.

I ran to switch my jean jacket for my formal show jacket, slammed my wooden top hat onto my head and put on my gloves. I was tapping my riding crop against the top of my boot to one of my favorite tunes when Sally led a fully-bridled Sultan out of the barn into the warm night air. With one final, deep breath, I stepped up to Sultan's side and was just admiring the way his black coat shimmered and his silky tail fell from its high arch when Sally grabbed my leg I had automatically bent, and boosted me into the saddle on the count of three. From that moment on all thoughts of shimmering coats and silky tails vanished from my mind. All I saw was the view from between Sultan's pointed ears. All I felt was power beneath me as he stepped out into a brisk walk, balanced and collected. All of my thoughts were focused on communicating to Sultan what I needed him to do at the moment.

We were soon at the entrance to the warm up ring, and then I guided him in and to the right along the rail. I shortened my reins about three inches and asked Sultan for a trot, sat the first few beats, and then began to post in rhythm with his movements. Our warm up was short as always, a spin both directions, keeping him as slow and relaxed as possible. It wasn't long before we were standing outside the main ring, pointed toward the in-gate. "Do not let him look at that grandstand. Focus his eyes where you want them. And keep those canter transitions slow! Keep your seat down and just pitter-patter your hands on the reins." Sally repeated all the things I already knew. "All right, you ready? I'm going to jazz him up a little going in that ring." Sally led Sultan forward, I clucked, he picked up the trot to which I sat. I bumped him back gently, and Sally clapped her hands as she jogged alongside of us. When we arrived closer to the ring I snapped my crop, clucked again and began posting. It was going to be good, I knew. He was attentive and listening. He was responsive. My only worry was that first canter transition, that left lead. When it was called for, I shifted my weight slightly, and touched with my leg and right rein.

"Canter," I said firmly, preparing for him to leap into it and dive against the bit. He didn't, and I almost smiled and laughed as he rocked gently beneath me, "just like an equitation horse," as Sally had always described his canter. Trotting into the line up I knew beyond a doubt that our class had gone well. "I think we've got it together now, boy," I whispered as I patted Sultan's neck in the line-up. Apparently the judge agreed because he pinned us first. Even our victory pass was good!

"And for your approval down victory lane in this Jr. Exhibitor 3 Gaited class, here is CH My Majesty and Maria Jones!" Ecstatic only begins to describe the look on my face when we trotted out of the ring.

"Finally," I murmured, hugging Sultan's now-sweaty neck. "We finally got it."

"Yes, you did." Sally patted my knee, "for now." She smiled. I sat up straight again and laughed because I knew it was true. There was always a new challenge when riding...especially when you were riding Sultan.

Chapter 16

When our little group arrived back at our barn I swung off, but was persuaded to remount for pictures. When the many camera flashes finally ceased, I dropped both stirrups, swung my right leg over the saddle, and landed hard on my flat riding boots. I was immediately surrounded by people hugging and congratulating me as Sultan was led away. My dad and Jessica were there. They had arrived in time for my class. I wanted to go tell Sultan what a good boy he was, but I was sort of stuck. Claire shoved her way through the little crowd and threw her arms around my waist. "He looked great!" she exclaimed.

"Thanks," I replied, smiling down at her. She'd become something like my little sister. "C'mon," I directed her, "let's go give this peppermint to Sultan." As we headed into the barn, her matching me stride for stride, I asked her if she was ready for tomorrow. She took a deep breath.

"Yes," she replied.

"Yes, but…?" I stopped in the aisle with a half smile and faced her.

"But what if he doesn't walk for me?" she asked.

"He'll walk," I said. "And if not, too bad. You sit up, and you say 'walk,' and hold him right to your seat. Just keep repeating walk to him. You make him walk. He'll walk. That's not what you're really worried about, though, is it?" She shook her head.

"No."

"You're worried about his leg." She nodded. I squatted down in front of her in the aisle, balancing myself there without touching the ground and getting my suit dirty. I suddenly felt inspired: words were just coming to me, and I didn't know why. So I said them. "Claire, he *wants* to show. His leg is fine. He wants to jump, but he can't jump because it's just too risky, so we made him Saddleseat because he is a show horse and he wants to perform. Sure, there's a risk in this, too. There's a risk in him being turned out in the pasture. There's a risk in him laying down in his stall and hurting himself getting up!

Sometimes little risks are worth it though. He's not worried. He wants to go out there tomorrow, and he wants to perform. Are *you* going to hold him back?" The girl raised her eyes to mine and shook her head.

"No," she replied.

"Good," I said briskly, and stood back up. "Let him show, Claire." I turned and continued to Sultan's stall, un-wrapping the mint in my hand. She followed one step behind.

I rolled over as the phone rang. Who was calling at—what time was it? It was the front desk, our wake-up call. My dad and Jessica were in a room across the hall, but I was staying with the Dormans so Emily and I could hang out together and talk all night (as long as we did it quietly so we didn't keep her parents up.) Mr. Dorman picked up the phone, thanked the person at the front desk, and called half-heartedly, "Time to get up, everyone!" No one moved for another two minutes or so, when Emily groggily threw her pillow at me, and then we both laughed and crawled out from under our covers. We took turns in the bathroom, and said we'd meet Mr. and Mrs. Dorman downstairs in the lobby. I yawned as we waited for the elevator.

"We could be down there already if we'd taken the stairs," I commented as it finally dinged and the door opened. We stepped inside and stood there for another two minutes as it waited for invisible people to board.

"I know," Emily said, "but what's the rush? My parents will be another 10 minutes anyway." We were groggy on the drive to the show, having been up until 12:30, but we were wide awake when we entered the barn once again.

Claire walked up to me in her off-green suit, everything but her jacket on. "I love that color," I said, reaching to straighten her tie. "Look at me," I commanded, examining her face. "Where's your make-up box?" She stepped to the nearest chair and handed it to me. I opened it up and added a touch more eye-liner to her left eye. "Perfect, you're gorgeous. Go find a crop." She did just that.

"Hey!" Sally greeted me as I strolled down to Major's stall. He was nearly ready to go, and Sally held his bridle in her hands. Claire was the third class. "I'm just waiting for the five minute call to the start of the show," she explained to me, glancing at my face and pausing there. "Man, you're going to need a lot of makeup tonight for your class. You look like the living dead. What were you doing last night?"

"Thanks, Sally." I laughed, "A little bit of everything, movies, popcorn, talking, reading, listening to music…"

"I hope you still have energy left to ride," Sally joked.

"Oh, I do." I assured her.

"Five minutes to show time, exhibitors. We'll be starting

off the day with our Lead-Line Walk Only class, followed by our Lead-Line Walk and Trot class. Next to show will be Walk and Trot Pleasure 12 and Under…" Sally was halfway through bridling Major by the time the announcer finished his speech. I watched from the aisle as she adjusted his cavesson and curb chain, and then led him out of the stall. Claire stood by the doorway all dressed up and ready, crop in hand. Sally halted Major just outside the barn and unrolled the stirrups. She raised his head and said, "Park out." Major stretched out into the correct position, making him lower to the ground and easier for Claire to mount. With a leg-up from Sally, Claire was in the saddle and gathering her reins. Sally checked quickly over everything and our little group made its way to the warm up ring for what seemed like the millionth time. I watched Claire with a smile and couldn't help but think how adorable she looked on the big liver chestnut. In the warm up ring, Sally told her to head to the rail the first direction and take Major around at a walk once to keep him settled. The gelding kept up a steady but eager gait, although I could see that he was enjoying the scenery and not paying much attention to his little rider. "Claire you can pick up a trot!" Sally called. The girl shortened her reins and asked Major to pick up the faster gait.

"Trot!" she commanded. Major sprang forward into his natural, flowing trot, and the two looked…

"Perfect, Claire. Just perfect!" Sally said. We stood there, an awed group in center ring, looking as if we'd seen a miracle, because we had. Major's movements were perfectly balanced, and he never missed a step. We were beyond thrilled. I'd done my job. Major was doing well again. He was happy. Claire had her horse to ride and show and care for. She was happy. There was only one piece missing from the puzzle, only one person who wasn't happy and her name was Carol. I knew that Sally had informed her of Major's first show. I saw her glancing toward the spectators along the rail every now and then, and I was sure I also knew who she was hoping to see. When Claire halted Major next to us, together Emily and I took down the horse's tail as Sally walked Claire through some last minute instructions. Yet I could tell that most of them were automatic, flowing only from years of sending horse and rider combinations into the show ring. Sally was giving her the generic run through; her mind was elsewhere. "And in the line-up what rein do you loosen up?" she asked the girl.

"The curb." Claire replied, also automatically.

"Very good," Sally responded, glancing around once again. "Let me see your line up pose." I really knew Sally was off somewhere else at the moment then, because this was a pleasure class. It didn't really matter if Claire's hands were up and heels were down or not, but Claire didn't seem to mind practicing. She raised her chin, stretched her heels down in the stirrups and set her hands beautifully. "Nice," Sally barely looked at her. She sighed, and then reached for Major's bridle. "Alright, let's move closer down to the ring." Our group began to walk forward. A big thrill ran through me watching Major's hooves carry him forward across the gravel and dirt. I had dreamed of this for so long it barely seemed real to me. How could it be? This was the broken, spiritless horse that had come to us a year ago. Yet, here he was, carrying his own weight and a little more with apparent ease and obvious happiness.

"You should have a nice class," Emily commented, glancing around at the five or so other walk-trotters. Claire nodded. She was now looking at the rail of the show ring. There were her parents in our box seats, my parents, Emily's parents, there was Tara her best friend, there was Holly, Valerie, and the rest of the barn crew…I could see the disappointment in Claire's face now, too. We all stood in disappointment.

"Walk and Trot Pleasure 12 and Under, we're ready for you in the ring. Come on in!" the announcer blared.

"Start him slow," Sally instructed. "Just sit the first few

beats." Determination crossed the girl's face, and as she sat and bounced she clucked to Major and drove him right up in that bridle. "Beautif…" Sally began, but stopped halfway through the word.

Something by the in-gate had caught her eye. I glanced up, as I ran along Major's right side. Walking toward the left hand side of the in-gate was a tall blonde woman. She paused to rest and leaned against the fence by the secretary's stand. Major raised his head and picked up the speed a little bit, when his eyes caught sight of her. He wasn't one for whinnying, but as he drew closer his body quivered and he let out a loud, ringing whinny.

"Trot!" Claire commanded, and tapped him with the crop in her hand, not seeing what was causing him to whinny. One more stride and they were in the ring. Sally, Emily and I stood together at the gate, eyes glued to Major for the first trip around the ring. After she saw that Claire was doing fine, though, Sally dashed off toward where that lady had been, the one who I was almost certain was Carol from the quick glimpse I'd gotten. Gosh, her ride was perfect. They walked. They trotted. They lined up. She loosened her curb, swiveled in the saddle and smiled at me. I gave her a thumbs up sign.

"And we have the results of class number 104, the Walk and Trot Pleasure 12 and Under….the winner of our class is number 88, Timeless, owned by Carol Lynn and ridden by Claire O'Daniel!" Of course, I cheered. Sally jumped the fence so she could enter the ring from where she was, instead of running back to the in-gate. The rest of the class was pinned and filed out one by one. Claire's picture was taken and Sally led Major by his bridle to the far end of the ring for the start of their victory pass. He began to trot. He wasn't hurting. He wasn't lame. He wasn't even off a bit. As I waited at the gate for the three of them, I felt someone move up on my left.

"Thanks for all your work with him." It was Carol,

addressing Emily and I.

"You're welcome," we replied in unison. Then we both jumped back as Major came charging out of the gate. Carol put a hand on Claire's knee and smiled.

"My dear, that was a beautiful ride." The girl beamed down at her.

"Thanks!" The rest of the walk back to the barn was in silence. Claire's parents were waiting there with cameras when we arrived, and we all posed in a group, then separately.

"You know, my doctor says I'm healthy enough to ride again," Carol announced. I froze from what I was doing. What if she wanted Major back to ride? What would we do then? After all that work...but he was her horse after all... "But I'm not ready to...not just yet. When I do start riding again, though, I doubt I'll be jumping. I love it, but my doctors wouldn't really approve. So I'll probably be back in the Saddleseat showring before too long. But I think Major is perfectly happy being a Walk and Trot horse, so I see no reason to change his life. He should stay where he is." Claire leaned down to hug Major's neck, and Carol stood watching with a smile. The first real smile I'd seen on her face since I'd met her.

"What can I say, you're a genius." Emily rested her elbow on my shoulder. A familiar feeling came over me. I knew it from somewhere before; but couldn't place it. "Reminds me of what we did with Triumph," Emily said. That was it. I'd felt this sense of completion with Triumph once my job with her was done. I looked at the girl and horse once more.

"It's only just beginning, kid!" Sally reached up and pulled Claire out of the saddle and into her arms to give her a hug. It was, indeed. Major had healed, and he'd proven to all who stood surrounding him now what Sally and I knew all along. Everyone could see that there was much ahead for our new pair, and for Carol as well, though a year before no one would've thought it possible. But you can't really blame them for doubting it. *It was quite amazing, and...unexpected. But, sometimes unexpected things happen, and the way they happen leaves awed onlookers standing in disbelief. This was, indeed, one of those times.*